Table of contents

Forward/Dedication	i
Chapter 1: Dying	1
Chapter 2: 1974	4
Chapter 3: Dying part 2	12
Chapter 4: 1966	16
Chapter 5: Dying part 3	24
Chapter 6: 1980	28
Chapter 7: Dying part 4	39
Chapter 8: 1984	44
Chapter 9: Dying part 5	55
Chapter 10: 2012	60
Chapter 11: Dying part 6	71
Chapter 12: 1987	75
Chapter 13: Dying part 7	87
Chapter 14: 2018	91
Chapter 15: Dying part 8	102
Chapter 16: 2002	106
Chapter 17: Dying part 9	118
Chapter 18: 2019	122
Chapter 19: Revelations	135
Chapter 20: Rebirth	140
Chapter 21: Remembrance	146

Forward/Dedication

Sometimes the events of our lives seem like the biggest moments that we will ever see as they happen. Other times the mundane day to day lulls us into a sublime submission without direction. No matter what happens, when life draws to a close, what moments will be the ones you choose to remember? This book is dedicated to the friends that have inspired me, the family that has loved me, and those that have come in and out of my life to help me find direction.

The Scent of White

The Scent of White
Chapter 1: Dying

The sterile stench of white entered my lungs in the first breath I could remember. Breath. It's the simplest thing in the world, so why does it feel like so much work. A single breath entering the body and all the waste leaving from our existence in one affirming breath. Why is it so hard?

Blinding Light.

Doctors?

Nurses.

Noise. That incessant beeping that will not leave my head.

I am so thirsty. Maybe some water will help. It always does. We are bathed in it. It centers us. Calms nerves. "Water" Why is no one bringing me water? "WATER" They must hear me. People are everywhere. They seem excited. Running in their predetermined order. Damn them. Just get my water and it will be fine. Enough of this, I will get it myself.

Why can't I move? Come on just a little. Arms. Legs. Something. All I want is a glass of water. I must be able to do this. There is no reason. I didn't do anything. I am fine. Just bring me a cool, crisp glass and it will all be over. I will tell you, stop running around. Just see me. Come on see me. Such a simple request. "WATER!"

Am I dead? Is this what the great here-after feels like? Watching. If this is heaven, it is one cruel joke. I can't be dead. I was just outside with Ranger. Cool fall wind. There is no way I am dead. I can't be dead; nobody moves for the dead. These people can't hold their feet still. There wouldn't be a fuss over me if I was dead. Just pull up the sheets and punch the clock. There must be more. Always something more.

Voices. I hear voices. What are they saying? Focus. There has to be a reason I am here. I can hear them, but why can't I make them out? Are they talking to me? That nurse looks like she wants something. But what is it? FOCUS. If I can just figure this out, I am sure it will all be fine. Where the hell is that water? Something. Just give me something to hold onto.

"Can you understand me Mr..." Wait. What was that? I almost had it that time. "Mr. Larkin, do you understand?" I HEARD her. "Yes. YES! I understand you." Why does she have that blank stare? Couldn't she hear me? I can hear my voice. She must hear me. "YES, I AM HERE" Nothing. Why is there nothing? Come on just give me something. A drink will clear up my voice. Please. Just a sip, something to clear my head, clear my voice.

The Scent of White

People. STOP! I know you are doing something. You always are. People moving about. Simple tasks to be done but stop for one second and see me. I am right here. I am trying to communicate with you damn people. I am talking. I am trying to move. Why am I being held down? Why can't you hear me? I don't recognize any of you. Maybe if you knew me. I mean really KNEW me you would stop you running and know what I need. Come on you. The nurse. I am right here. Yea you. The one asking me the questions. You saw me for a second. Stop and see me again. Bring me that water. I am begging you. Just for a minute.

Tired. I am so tired. All this fighting with you. All this struggle. I just want to be done. Stop it for a minute. Keep up the work you were determined to finish. It is fine. I will just lay here. I know you don't mean to ignore me, but you are. I can't keep pace with you. I am an old man. It tires me out just watching you. Maybe if I am able to just rest for a minute you will be done, and you will stop for me. That is all I need. Just a minute of your time. A cool drink. A clear head. Maybe we can get on with it then. Maybe it will all be clear. You keep going. I am just going to lay here for a moment and close my eyes. Don't worry about me. I will be alright, just a little rest.

Chapter 2: 1974

High school is miserable. It doesn't matter if you are on top of the social ladder or the bottom. A bunch of pubescent kids trying to figure life out. Pretending to be confident, strong individuals but not being able to comprehend a single thing outside of the little box that they are placed in. We grow. We dream. We normalize. The winds of change never blow quite as fierce as they do during that short period of our lives.

Scott Larkin bounded up the steps. Half full of excitement, half of fear. This was it. The first day that would change the rest of his life. The years where he would make his mark. The first day of high school. The scent of fall was in the air even though the summer heat of 1974 had put water restrictions on the whole town and sent near mass chaos when electricity was being regulated like gas at the pumps a few years before. This was the breath of fresh air that every person in town needed, the promise of renewal.

"Hey Scotty, how was your summer?" A familiar face, Julie Scooner, beamed as she walked up the stairs. Ah Julie. Every boy's dream girl, but for some reason she always took the time out for Scott. If this was the start of high school, he knew that it was going to be great. The year he could leave behind the awkward happenstance of middle school and come to grips with

The Scent of White

being a near-adult. Life really didn't get much better than this.

"Not too bad Jules. It sure would have been nice to spend more time at the lake... you know this heat and all. How was yours?" Great. The prettiest, smartest girl in the school and he started his first conversation of being a man making small talk about the weather. It didn't matter. She smiled, and to Scott that smile melted away all the insecurities he may have had about what lay before him. Maybe it was whole new world.

The doors to the school always seemed to whine when the kids opened them. Almost wishing that they would stay away and just let the old building rest in peace. But as Scott and Julie entered the building that day the sound welcomed them to a hallway of fresh paint, clean floors, and hundreds of faces. And as they piled in, filed one by one, the halls once again filled with laughter, youth, and childish glee that, while fleeting, made the 1974 school year one to remember.

Every school year the start feels like it passes uneventfully. Friends came. New friends were made. Classes started and classes ended. There is a certain solace in the monotony of everyday life that comes from a rigid schedule, and Scott fell into the rhythm with each of his peers. As the leaves changed and the weather cooled you could sense the freedom and excitement fading, showing up in solid bursts instead of a murmur, and the schedule of life moving along its path.

Football season was the real start of fall for Scott. Tryouts brought together all the friends new and old. "Hey Scotty, you trying out for receiver again?" Trevor's voice always boomed over the others in the locker room. "Of course." Most of the football team had graduated the year before, so while there were no guarantees, Scott felt he had a good chance of at least marking one of the starting positions with his name. But at this point, anything would be better than being the water boy again. The entire junior varsity season he had to do double duty, play receiver for JV football and be the varsity student assistant, better known to the team as the waterboy. Those things happen when your dad is a volunteer coach. Football was freedom. A break from school, a break from homework, and a break from home. While each of those things were good in their own right, the game was school yard fun coupled with Friday night lights.

Scott did make receiver. Second string backup. While Julie tried to reassure him that it was a great start, he always felt like he failed to seize his

The Scent of White

opportunity to start three years on the varsity team. There were no great victories to be that year. The team finished the season 8 and 8 and just missed the play offs. Disappointment filled air in the Lockerroom after the season, no matter how short lived the self-pity was. Days turned to weeks, and weeks turned to months and time turned the disappointment of the season into a faded memory as new opportunities arose.

By winter break, a thick white layer of snow covered most of the northland. The Midwest always seemed to stall this time of year. No one venturing out into the minus twenty-degree weather unless it was absolutely called for. Scott and his friends were some of the few brave souls who would venture out from time to time to try their hand at fishing on the frozen pond, blasting haphazardly down a snow-covered hill, or gliding across the local hockey rinks. But for the rest of the town, time stood still in a paused existence waiting for spring to breathe life into their veins again.

The only break for the longevity of winters grasp, would be the holidays. A big meal with family near and far for Thanksgiving. Gifts and cheer for Christmas. And a celebration of new life as the year turned the page. "What do you want for Christmas hun?" Scott's mom Sarah always had his wishes and desires in mind. What did he want? That was always the hardest question for him. While other kids seemed to have lists, dream gifts, Scott never really knew what he wanted. Sure, there were a lot of things that he would like. But how do you ask for them? How do you figure out what you really want? And what if you don't get them, isn't that just setting up for disappointment?

For Christmas that year he did get two gifts that would stay with him for the rest of his life. Being 15 in the northern Midwest, he was way past due to get a knife of his own. But that year under the tree was a trapper Buck knife with his name plastered all over it. His grandpa would also hand down a watch that he received for Christmas nearly 60 years before. A simple inscription on the back 'put your faith in family and family in faith'. Simple things always had the ability to outlast the most elaborate charades of grandeur.

As 1974 faded into 1975 not much would change. It would be the year Scott lost his grandfather, even though it was expected, the shockwave reverberated with him for years. The school year would drag on. After the holidays there isn't much to look forward to in high school. Students would try to do their best work, even at last minute. The snow would melt. Frozen ponds would turn to open water ripe for summer fishing.

The Scent of White

Spring break signified two things to the students; the last leg of the school year was about to start, and the endless winter would give way to the fresh air and warm winds of the changing season. Scott knew that spring would bring changes. He would complete his first year of real school. His first 'adult' job would be right around the corner. A summer of fishing and camping with his family. Breaks of swimming and just hanging out at the lake with friends. The nights would grow long, and freedom would be born again.

Spring also brought about baseball. If football marked the start of fall, baseball was the birth of a whole new season. Tryouts signified the start of the season like no other event could do. Spring ball promised warmer days, friendships to be solidified in play, and the end of the school year.

Scott always played the same position since little league. He was a solid second baseman. Even as a sophomore he knew that he would start. If it hadn't been for a few seniors playing their last season, there was even talk of him starting varsity as a freshman. But baseball was also a release. After months in the cold and unyielding winter, you could spend more time in the great outdoors and enjoy the relighting of all your senses.

The team did great again this year. Making it all the way through the section finals. Their hope of a state title was not to be in the spring of 75. It is always harder for a small school in the north to compete with the bigger schools, especially when your season is a month shorter in the north. There is only so much you can do in a gym. In the end, it was a success, not just for the team but the whole school. Regardless of the sport, students seem to draw much pleasure about being a part of the festivities and games.

As the last days of school drew to a close, Scott finally gained the courage to ask Julie out. The thought of a first date both made his heart race, and time stand still as he awaited her answer. Scott had butterflies, nerves, excitement. It is something that we never seem to lose, even as we age, the promise and desire that comes with starting something new. But if the date was a big deal, the first kiss could have sparked a fire the likes the world had never saw. This was the year for him. A kiss can always be the promise of a relationship. The tingling of lips. The passion of someone else feeling more about you then you knew was possible. The insecurities fade into a relevance in our lives. Scott felt every one of those emotions and knew he was forever changed because of it.

The Scent of White

The romance was short-lived, as first love can be fickle and fleeting. Regardless, it was his first. While any adult would make an argument of what love really is, for Scott this would without question be first love. How could it not. The first kiss. The first date. The first loving caress from someone else. Each one of those things change you. And even while we grow and each emotion deepens and begin to understand them on a level so much deeper, the start of a love map begins somewhere, and for him, this was it.

Chapter 3: Dying, part 2

God I am so tired. Why is it every time I wake up from a solid nap that I feel this way? My eyes are so heavy. I can't open them. Why can't I open them? I have never been this tired.

There we go. Light. Where the hell am I? Machines. The damn beeping. That can't be my alarm clock. It isn't right. Something isn't right. Focus. Alright, I can start to see again. Where am I? I am so thirsty. I could really use some water. I must get up. Why won't my body work.

More light. There we go. Here it comes. What is this place. I have to see something. Something I recognize. Who is that? Ah; I remember now, hospital. Still no idea why I am here. It is coming back now. At least I can see.

They are not running anymore. Is that good? Is it bad? I wish they would stop and see me. Still working. It feels like I am not here. Why? They are good people, that I know. But why don't they see me? The doctor does nothing but focus on me, but he can't see through the issue in front of him, not me. This is different, right? What is going on?

The nurse, is she talking again '...I think...awake'. Wait. Can I hear something again? Come

The Scent of White

on focus. I still need that water. That would help. '...doctor he is awake' SUCCESS! I heard that. I am awake. Why wouldn't I be awake? Yes. Yes. I am awake. Can't you hear me? YES, I am awake!

'Mr. Larkin, I am doctor Kraft. Can you hear me?' YES, I can hear you. 'Mr. Larkin, do you understand me?' YES, I understand you damn it. Do I hear myself? I shouldn't have to think this hard. I must be speaking. I know I can hear me.

'Mr. Larkin, can you blink?' Blackness. There it is. I must have blinked. Everything went dark. 'Mr. Larkin, I am not sure if you can hear me or not. It's a good sign your eyes are moving, how much you can understand I don't know. But I need to tell you something.' I didn't blink? He couldn't see? Of course, my eyes are moving. I am looking at you, aren't I?

Give me some water first. Just a taste. It will calm me. I need it. I am so thirsty. Please. Just a little comfort first. 'Mr. Larkin, you have been in a coma. You have been out for the last six days. We are still not sure why or how yet, although we have a good idea, we are hoping soon you can help fill us in...'

Wait, WHAT? A coma? Is that why I can't move? I thought a coma was supposed to be a long sleep. Like don't you wake up and just walk out of here? Isn't that how it works? I have to be fine. I am sure I couldn't have been doing anything big. I remember being outside on a walk.

'...we know a few things Mr. Larkin. We know you were out walking your dog. And this is where we are not sure what exactly happened. At this point you are exhibiting all the signs of a stroke, and all the testing point to that as well. We believe you had a short-term blocked artery that caused low blood flow to your brain. While it is fairly rare, this can cause a coma.'

A stroke? So now I am paralyzed. I thought that was only one side. That is recoverable. I will be fine. It might take a while, but there is always people who have had multiple. I have never had any heart conditions before. This must be just a hiccup. It will get better.

'As I was saying Mr. Larkin. We have been able to run some tests while you were out. There is a blockage in your heart. For now, I will just say it is significant. I have gone over this with your wife, but I will save you the stress of the details for now. We can't perform surgery until you are stronger. So, for now we are going to make sure you get plenty of rest. Your family is in the other room. Why don't you get some rest for now, and I will bring in your family soon.'

The Scent of White

Family. Yes, my family. They will understand. They are always the most important. All I really need is some water. Forget the rest. I will be fine. I am not that tired. Just bring me some water and let me see them. That is what I need. Just to connect with someone again.

My eyelids are heavy. Why? I am awake. I just felt awake. All I need is that damn water and to see something that is familiar. Family. I know he said family. That has always been the most important thing in my life. There can be no wrong in that. It will be better. It must be better. They know me. They know what to do. I know they will. I am fading. So fast. I must stay up and see them. I must fight this. But I am fading. Fading...

Chapter 4: 1968

There is a time in every child's life where they are fearless. They have not yet learned the rational and irrational fears that seem to come as a part of growing up. They aren't insecure. They know they can do anything. They are indestructible. But it can be a cruel trick of the mind the first time a child finds the invincibility they feel is not always the case.

The summer of 1966 was not unlike any other summer. Of course, each summer has its own adventures, weather, stories, and life events. For Scott, 1966 would be the year that his invincibility would get tested for the first time.

The weather was cool that summer. So, while kids played at the lake and partook in all the summer activities that you would expect, there was less time spent around the water than other years.

For an eight-year-old boy, it didn't matter where you were at. The summer meant no school, friends-a-plenty, and time that was just meant for yourself. At eight years old, there was a little more freedom from under a mother's watchful eye. Of course, she was still there, still knowing everything that you would be doing. But at the same time, there was

The Scent of White

more time where mom's attention would be distracted, and that is where a young boy's fun really began.

The start of the summer was filled with playing at the sand lot with his friends. A baseball game that never seemed to end. Somedays it was only 4 or 5 players. Somedays there would be enough for two whole teams! Little league started at the beginning of summer, but even with schedules being a part of each day, kids always found a way to the lot for just a little more.

Fishing trips with dad where always big events too. Even when they couldn't go as often as Scott wanted, there was always time to head to the lake. There was something about when a dad can spend time just focused on their child that makes them feel special. And these trips always held a special place in Scott's heart. This was his introduction to a lifetime love of fishing.

By the 4th of July, Scott had already amassed a fortune of experiences and fun summer activities. Though if you asked his mom, his constant response was 'I'm bored.' But like with any child, the days were filled with adventure and the nights only ended by the porch light, selectively turned on by mom at the same time each night. The 4th of July was the biggest event of the summer. Family would all gather. There would be a meal to beat all the rest of the summer, of course only with the best bar-b-que. Mouth wateringly sweet, fresh off the coals meat and veggies that would make anyone's appetite go into overdrive. But most of all, it was always spent on the lake. Swimming, skiing, playing and enjoying the little things with family.

Shortly after the 4th, IT happened. The events of that day would be burnt into the very depths of his mind. Scott headed out the door bright and early. Mom's last words of warning, "Scotty, be careful. Remember you have to be home before practice!" It was no different than any other time he left the house. However, this was going to be the day that his group of friends finally climbed the widow-maker.

The widow-maker was a big hundred-year-old white pine that shadowed the backyards of several of the houses in the neighborhood. The older boys would tell stories of kids falling to their emanate doom just by making it up to the first tier of branches. Of course, this was coupled with tales of a dad going to retrieve a wayward frisbee and falling making his wife a widow. So, the widow-maker was undeniably irresistible to an adventurous eight-year-old boy or girl. Scott was no different, he was going to concur that tree and see the entire town from the tippy top.

The Scent of White

As the boys gathered, the first two Ryan and Jake, suddenly weren't feeling so good. It is amazing how fast injuries and illness can happen when death is on the doorstep. A couple more boys chickened out just on face value alone. But that would stop Scott, his best friend at the time Mike, and Darrel from reaching the top. It was beautiful. Limbs bigger than most tree trunks and tons of spots just begging for a treehouse. After 5 minutes the boys had reached a level where earth and sky felt like it collided. After 5 more they would be high enough to see the roof tops of all the neighborhood. Darrel stopped halfway up that climb, "Guys, I am just going to sit here for a minute. You know check out that spot for our fort."

A quick breeze shook the tree, seemingly from its very roots. That little breeze was enough to make the boys feel that pit in their stomach tell them they might have had enough… well at least for today. There were more days to touch the sky and the heavens. It was time, they had enough. The trip down seemed so easy. No crawling looking for the next best spot. Just a quick hop from branch to branch until they would be safely grounded again.

On the way down, Scott misjudged a branch when he was only 10 feet from that sweet dirt below him. The sound would never leave his ears. Bark being stripped away from the branch in a sickening ripping fashion, the poof of air being driven from his lungs as his back caught a limb, and the final dead thump as his body hit the ground. This was sure death. It was the widow-maker after all. And then the searing pain shooting up his right arm was all he could feel.

All the boys scatted as young boys are known to do when big trouble is on the horizon. But not Mike. Mike was his best friend after all. Scott could feel the tears streaming from his eyes. Ashamed. Even at that age, Scott knew boys were supposed to be tough, not cry when something went wrong. Well that is what he thought anyway. But no matter how hard he fought, his tears could not be held back. "Jesus Scotty, look at your arm... it's... It's... It's just hanging there" Mike could barely stutter out the sentence as though the cat really did get his tongue this time. Scott couldn't look down. He knew that after this they would have to cut it off. After the pain he felt, there was no way they could save his arm. Even without looking, something that hurt that bad had to be taken off.

"I'll get your mom." As Mike called it out and scampered off all Scott could think was NO, not her. Anything but that. He would be forbidden to leave the house forever, not to mention what his father would

The Scent of White

say. Forget his arm this was the end of his life. But after waiting for what felt like hours but actuality was only a couple minutes, he could see HER coming up the path. "Scott, Scotty are you okay honey?" Well at least it wasn't yelling right now.

It was obvious, his arm was broke. Hanging there limp and at a 45-degree angle from the rest of his arm. In those days, ambulances were not the first thing that you could or would call. Instead he was loaded up into the neighbor's station wagon and off to the hospital they went. Even while terrified about being the one arm man, anything would be better than the agony he was currently in.

At the hospital it seemed like all focus was on him. The nurses hovered, the doctor approached with a crooked smile and a knowing look. This surely wasn't the first broken arm any of them had seen, but it must have been the worst. In his mind it had to be the worst anyway. He had no way of knowing the doctor would see a precarious youth at least once a month who gotten into a situation that caused lifetime memories of broken bones, twisted limbs, and injuries of all shapes and sizes. The doctor's crooked smile giving away that this was almost a rite of passage for these kids.

After some attention, a plan for fixing him up, an x-ray, a sweet grape sucker, and a tussle of the hair, Scott was sent home with his arm bandaged to three times its normal size and a plan for surgery as soon as the swelling released some of its hold on his arm.

Scott did end up in a cast. One that would last six weeks and take up the majority of his summer. There were checkups. Showers were filled with bread bags and rubber bands over his arm. His buddies would be at the lake swimming feeling the cool crisp water on the warmest of the summer days while he was stuck inside or sitting on the beach. A broken bone might have been a rite of passage, but to him it was the end of the summer.

Dad still took him fishing, even though he could hardly handle the rod. His family tried hard to find some fun summer activities that were fun, but little league was over, his favorite things were sidelined, and it all weighed heavy. While he could not play ball, he elected to play manager for the rest of the summer. The adventures seemed to abruptly halt, even when he was included. Turns out the widow-maker claimed another victim, a young boy's summer.

Being right-handed wasn't so bad over the summer, but the cast would be off before school barely got going. There goes the only advantage of being in a

The Scent of White

cast for a boy of his age, he would still be able to write. When some children see behind the veil of invincibility, their fearlessness if forever changed. Yet others like Scott only have a scare. That is why he would always think 'one day, one day I will beat the widow-maker and make it to the top'. Though that day would never come, it would be the first nemesis he could own completely. It would also mark the point that while only scarred, now he could feel the pit in his stomach with each daring, adrenaline filled decision he made. That pit would form in the very bottom of his stomach. Of course it wouldn't prevent stupid ideas or actions, but it would be there. The first realization that maybe he wasn't quite as bullet proof as he thought.

Chapter 5: Dying, part 3

Oh, I hurt. So much. Each muscle in my body feels like it is on fire. Like it is eating itself. What is going on? Why do I feel like this? My eyes are so heavy. I just need to get them to open.

Bright. It is so freaking bright in here. I can't see a thing. Just white. The sanitary white smell that is only comes from far too many cleaning chemicals mixed with new sterile products being moved about.

A Hospital. That is where I am. Come on eyes, focus. Blurry. Everything is blurry. All I can remember is thirst. That great thirst that still hasn't gone away. Hasn't someone brought me water yet? Why am I here again? I know I talked to the doctor. Give me a minute. Walking, I remember that. I remember the crisp air. Oh, so good. But not now. Focus. What did he say? Coma. That's right I have been here for a week. Stroke. I think there was something about that. Surgery. Again. I have had a few. Damn my brain, I must be able to put this together. What was that last thing? That seemed important. Why can't I just remember?

FAMILY. That was it. He was going to get my family. Finally. Some comfort. I miss them. I need them. The damn water can wait. Bring them to me. That is all I

The Scent of White

really need. My hurting body and weak mind can take comfort in them. Just bring them to me.

There. I can see those shapes. Why is it taking so much longer for my eyes to open? Last time they didn't shoot open, but it sure didn't take this long. Is my brain getting weaker? Am I dying? I can't think about that. All I need is to see THEM. The only thing that makes this world go around for me. I just want them.

A little more. Starting to focus. Even as a blurry outline I can tell. That chair to my left. There is no way I can mistake that. Sweet, beautiful Mary. It only makes sense she would be the first thing I see. She always has been the clarity. For the first time I can remember since getting stuck in here I am at least feeling some relief. My muscles aren't quite as sore. Oddly even my thirst seems to be quenched, if even just a little.

To her left, there she is. Heather. My second born. She was always my daddy's girl. I don't see Ryan though. Maybe he's down the hall. For a son in law, he definitely isn't the worst she could do. Never good enough for my little girl, but he tries and treats her like a queen should be treated. I give him all the credit for that.

Where is he? He must be here. The door. He is always by the door. My boy. Frank. My first born. Just need to look for the door. There he is. I knew he would be here. I bet he left Lindsey at home. She isn't delicate, but I know that he would want to shield his wife from this. At least for now. He is always here. As I have gotten older, I would never admit it, but I have relied on him. On his visits. Often giving him projects to "keep him busy and not bored" but that we both know I can't do it alone anymore. He will be the rock when I am not there.

Wow. For a minute, if just a minute, I am not worried about this. Hell, even if I don't know what this is, it doesn't concern me much right now. Their worried looks tell me I should be worried. But right now, all I can think about is them. I wonder if I am smiling. I can feel my smile on the inside. They are here. And that is all that matters. Even dying to quench my dry throat is a second thought.

I just woke up. Why are my eyes getting heavy again? My heart is full. I know I have thought that a lot over the years. But this time I can feel it. My heart feels full. If I could talk the smart ass side of me would blame it on the blockage. It isn't. It is family. They fix things. They take care of things. They are here for me. There is nothing that can tear them away. I appreciate that.

The Scent of White

So tired. This is different. Last time I fought it. I needed. I wanted. But right now, right now I feel nothing but rest. I am relaxed. Maybe this time I will rest. Maybe my eyes won't be so heavy when I wake up. Maybe it will be fixed. They will fix it. I know when I wake up there will be more. It will be better. Just a little more rest.

Chapter 6: 1980

There are moments in life that are defining. Even though we don't know it at the time, the course of our life is altered forever just by chance. 1979 happened to be one of those years for Scott.

It started off as a carefree year, as many of years for young men. Scott had just started his second year of learning a trade. Originally, he had intended to go to college and take on the 70s vibes just like all the other graduates he knew. That would have been an adventure. He looked forward to coeds, parties, classes, and everything that comes when you live on a residential college campus. He had even applied and was accepted to the University of Michigan. It was a dream come true. 8 hours away. No parental supervision. Everything he wanted to prove he was an adult.

Scott didn't come from a rich family. They were doing fine, living in a good neighborhood, all their needs taken care of. But when it came to college, the answer was simple, there was no extra money. After a lot of deliberation and some long tear-filled nights, he knew his dream of Michigan wasn't the best choice. It just didn't make sense. Go deep into debt for an adventure with his friends or stay home and learn a trade and start making money. A bachelor's degree could always wait.

The Scent of White

The summer of 1978 he made his choice, he would go to the local trade school and start learning and apprenticing to be an electrician. There was a need. Minimum wage was $2.68 but as an electrician he would easily make $5 an hour or more depending on where he worked. It was an easy decision, and after he had a conversation with his parents and the local school counselor is plan was set. Learn a trade. Get a job. Start living the dream.

This decision wasn't his life altering moment, no, that moment came almost two years later in 1980. There were a lot of big moments at school and choosing a career does alter the direction of your life, but it is so small in the big picture of who we are. The real moment came about 2 weeks after he started that second year of trade school. That is when he first saw her. Mary.

Scott was doing what he usually did, hanging out with other electric students, talking about the trade, talking about girls, and solving the world's problems one talk at a time. They always seemed to gather in the same spot. Far end of the courtyard, right under the oldest Elm tree on campus. The few guys that smoked grass could get away with it. There were enough trees to shade you from the late fall heat. It was a nice spot.

That day, there was something different. A dusty hair, green eyed girl seemed to be stumbling down a path rarely taken. She looked lost. She looked frightened, well maybe no frightened but nervous at the lest. She must be new to the school. When Scott looked up, he could not take his eyes from her. She seemed soft and innocent. Not the usual girls taking the secretarial program or court reporting programs offered at the school. She was different. Before he could even think of saying hi, one of the girls hanging out had ran over to give her a hand. A lost opportunity. A moment that could not be lived again.

That one simple event, seeing someone for the first time, that would be the moment that would alter the stars in Scott's world. He wouldn't learn that yet. He wouldn't even really understand it for quite a long time. This wasn't a love at first sight moment. Maybe it was, but it wasn't a moment that either would ever realize. She even faded from his mind a bit aside from a random thought until they officially met two months later. There was always a huge campus Halloween party where most of the student body would attend for a while before wandering off to other, less appropriate parties.

Mary walked in. Still looking as innocent as ever, but there was an air of confidence to her this time.

The Scent of White
She belonged there now, and she knew it. A couple of hours had passed with the usual Halloween fair and games. Mary had dressed up as Little Bo Peep, her favorite character from all her childhood memories. Scott was Súperman, but to be fair so where about 10 of the guys at the party. The show was new, and everybody seemed to be in love with the comics.

Their chance meeting was more innocent than a usual hello. Mary had been walking by and stumbled. As fate would have it, that stumble was right into Scott walking the opposite direction. He didn't catch her, not even close to being that smooth or scripted out of a romantic movie. Instead, Mary bounced off his right shoulder and popped right back to her feet. Without missing a beat her head went straight toward the ground as she mumbled a shy 'sorry'. Technically that would be their first words. But the word Scott would never forget is the one that followed. He had put his hand on her shoulder, to help stabilizer, but with a tenderness that showed no remorse either. Mary looked up with her bottom lip between her teeth and said "hi". That was the moment.

Certain conversations just never seem to end, even in the tough times, the angry times, the sad times, the one thing that stays is the conversation. It takes two remarkable people, or one astounding connection, to keep that conversation going. With Scott and Mary there was no try. It was as natural if they had been doing it their entire lives. And it was the conversation that would last the rest of their lives.

That first night, after the hellos and awkward introductions, they spent most of the night talking about their lives. Nothing was hidden. They talked about who they were. They talked about hopes. They talked about dreams. They told secretes that no one else knew. That first night they ditched their plans and their friends, just to talk until long after the campus parties were over. They went to the local diner for a malt and a basket of fries. Even the best moments need to come to an end, and at three in the morning they would call it a night. Not long before the sun would be up, and with tired eyes, they both knew the time had come for this moment.

After that first night, that conversation would continue. It continued nearly every night. Sometimes it would be just like the first night and carry on until the wee hours of the morning, and other times responsibilities ended it much earlier. It didn't matter if they were together or on the phone, the conversation would continue as if they didn't have a conscious choice in the matter. It was a reaction. It was a meeting of

The Scent of White

souls. Even though Scott didn't believe in fate until that day, from that moment on he knew that there were things in life that had to happen.

Throughout the entire fall Scott and Mary would only miss each other a handful of times. Some trips home, some events that couldn't be missed, schedules. That was the only silence either would go through at the end of the day. Even though some people may not have believed it to be a story book romance, to them it was the story of a life time and it was the one story they would tell each other over and over again, even while they were living it.

He would catch himself staring at her from time to time. She would never admit it, but the long stares from everyone she encountered belied her thoughts on how attractive she was. But that is not what would draw his attention for hours on end. For him, it was the way she carried herself. He would watch how her eyes would sparkle when she saw something new. He loved taking in the picture of her presentation and the aura of her being. For him, that inner beauty shined so much deeper than the physical attributes that people lust after.

By early that spring, Scott knew that she was the adventure that would last his lifetime. Anyone could clearly see that they were headed toward the church aisle. The looks they shared, and their smiling eyes were plenty for a complete stranger to know it. You would need to be blind to not see it happening. The event that solidified those thoughts for Scott, was the night that she was called home. It was a call that highlighted who she was deep down.

The family dog, chase, was dying. While that might seem trivial to some or feel like an expected part of life to others, for her it was an earthquake. Growing up with an animal as long as Mary could remember, made an impact. Scott had met her family a few times and felt like they all got along well. Mary begged him to come. She didn't need to beg, he would have followed her anywhere, but she needed him. Without a second thought, they were in the car and on the way.

Watching her tender care with chase as he was drawing the last breath he would ever take and feeling her strength and tenderness as she comforted her family was inspiring. Against all odds, she was the glue that held them together. It was then he knew. This woman would always be his strength, be by his side, show caring and compassion, and build a world that would not be matched.

Scott was a traditionalist by nature. When he was ready to purpose it was only right that he ask her

The Scent of White

father's permission. His hands were sweating the entire way out to the house. Her dad's smile as he pulled up set his nerves at ease. After a short discussion, the answer was clear to him to, the permission he sought was absolutely given.

The engagement was a simple affair. They didn't have much money. They were just starting out. Instead of purposing with fancy flowers, a several course meal, or all the charades that are expected in modern times, Scott simply invited her over for a night of being together. They spent the evening talking and laughing, eating junk food, and genuinely enjoying sharing the same air. As the night wore on, he found the nerve and the urge was more than he could bare. He got down on one knee, looked deep into her eyes, and simply said 'marry me'. There never was a moment of hesitation.

The rest of the evening was spent with vinyl records playing on the stereo, a six rack on the table, and spinning around and around in each other's arms until their legs could take no more. It was magical. Simple. Easy. It was the time of their lives. Each knew they were strong independently, and only stronger together.

We take so much time in planning big affairs when it comes to weddings. Most weddings could reach the thousands of dollars. Everyone they knew invited all the family and friends that they could think of. But in 1980, for a young couple just getting started, a wedding was a simple affair. They were engaged in March and planned for a fall wedding in September. The leaves would be changing in the Midwest and the winds would be perfect. Scott's friend had a barn turned storage that was perfect for hosting the few family and friends that lived close enough to come celebrate with them. The wedding would be done at Mary's church she attended since youth. It would be simple, beautiful and perfect.

Regardless of how much both Scott and Mary looked forward to being husband and wife, the wedding was not what mattered most to them. Their souls had been connected since long before. The marriage was just a formality. By that time, they had grown together so much and learned about each other, neither could imagine nor want a life apart. A life where they couldn't share all that made each other so unique was not a life they would chose to live in a thousand sunsets.

The first year was tough. So was the second. There is always an adjustment period living with someone new. A period where all that you knew about the other person is put into hyperdrive as you have all

The Scent of White

your daily habits merge and learn of the little things hidden behind closed doors. Scott and Mary had some adjustments getting used to each other. That is expected, but that is not what made it tough. Being a young couple with budding careers an only an inkling of directions is what made it tough. Scott graduated but was still apprenticing, which made money tighter than they would like. Mary had graduated with a secretarial degree but could only find temporary jobs for the first year. Stress comes from finding out all of the challenges that lay before a couple and having to endure together. In the end, that stress helped them learn to rely on each other for support and to stand by each other even on the hardest days.

Humble beginnings allow for appreciation when each part of a dream is realized. Scott and Mary had the same dream. It seems like such a cliché, the two-story house, a white picket fence, two kids, a dog. The old fashion American dream. The simplicity of the dream may make it seem obtainable and more of an old fashion statement to simpler times. There was also comfort in a dream of living a life full of faith, family, freedom, and friends.

The promise of hope gave them the confidence to live for their dream. By the third year of marriage they had worked, saved, and aimed for that goal. Mary had landed a great secretarial job at the local law firm. Scott had become a master electrician, and their days were filled with hard work. Their nights were filled with working together on projects, building a life, and finding the little things that make life special.

At the end of that third year, the stress and work had paid off. They had enough saved up to buy a little chunk of land outside of town, just big enough to have a little hobby farm and build the home they always wanted. They planned and worked, they toiled and dreamed. Through it all they became closer and more determined. This isn't to say there wasn't hard times. Sickness, arguments, challenges, the storms of life that you can either face head on looking for the slivers of light or crumble apart. For them, it was all a part of building a foundation of stone that could not be shaken.

Walking through the hardest times can make each step forward be followed by three steps back. Hand-in-hand they chose to walk the steps together. After each step their confidence grew. And with these steps they were growing to fulfill even the biggest part of the dream, creating the family that they both had craved since the day they knew it would be forever.

The Scent of White
Chapter 7: Dying, part 4

Oh, my head. Damn this headache. This is new. I usually don't have issues waking up. Why is this time so much harder? I just don't understand it. What in the world is happening to me?

Take stock. Where am I? The hospital. That's right, I had a stroke. I can't move. At least I can focus now. A bit. I am pretty sure I have at least an idea of what is going on now. I know more than I knew last time, at least that is a start.

My hand is moving. I think I can feel it. But how? I can't move. I can't even get water. Tubes running everywhere. But my hand is still moving. I know it. Time to open my eyes. I need to see. Ouch. The light. If I thought my head hurt before, be damned now it is on fire. It takes so long to focus. Come on. I can feel the family that is here, I don't need to see for that. Maybe if I try hard enough I can see what the doctors are running on about now.

There it is. A little focus. I can hear the machines. There is no one there. Do they think I am dead? Where is everyone? A little more to the right. Still nothing. It is my right hand moving. It shouldn't be this hard to move my eyes. It shouldn't take this long. How can my hand be moving; how can I feel that? Wait, Heather is here. My daughter Heather. The sweet one. The nurturer. The care giver. It makes sense that she would be the one holding my hand. Eyes wet with tears. Sadness drenching her face.

Talk to me Heather. I can hear you. I wish I could tell you that. Can't you see it in my eyes. I am here. I am with you. Don't cry. I know you are sad, and I know that you are taking this the hardest out of everyone. It is in your soul; you are a tender soul. But it is ok. Just see me. Just look at me. You can see me in here and you can talk to me. Just talk.

Oh, your voice. From the moment you made your first sound, I loved that voice. So sweet and kind. You don't have to remind me; I remember that time I carried you into the house after you fell off your bike. And yes, I remember when your first boyfriend broke up with you and we stayed up late eating ice cream, watching bad movies, and talking it out. That is one of my favorite memories. I will never forget it.

I don't want to go either Heather. Can't you see that in my eyes. I want to stay here. I want to spend so many more days with all of you. I want to see my grandchildren be born and grow. I want to watch each step you take. I want to be your confidant and person you can go to for fatherly advice. I want all that too,

The Scent of White

honey. I am a rock. I will make it. Watch. I would get up right now and hug you if I could.

Move. Damn it. Move. All I have to do is get up. I can't believe no one has gotten me a drink. It must have been days. I will die from dehydration first. Maybe not. I have tubes going everywhere. Who knows what is in those things. Maybe I will never die. I could be stuck here inside myself, this husk of a body, for years. But I must get it together. For her. For them. For everyone. I know I can do it, but not quite yet.

Don't give up on me. Please. Don't give up. It will never get out hearing you say it. I know you love me. I know you care about me. Don't say it. Don't say goodbye. Do you know something that I don't know? Just have faith in me. I am strong, I can do this. You know that I can.

Heather, I know why you are the one that chose to stay here while I slept. You won't leave my side. I know this. You truly have always been there for me. I know that you are my child, but sometimes it feels like you are more of a care giver than I could ever be. You were always the first to come to anyone's aid. That is part of who you are.

There is a certain peace with you here. Holding my hand and looking at me. I know you can at least see me here. Know on some level that I am here. I know you can't see all of me. I can feel that. It's in your eyes, that look where you don't think I can hear you. There is so much sadness in your eyes, and I would take it away if I could. I really would. You don't need to feel this way. Really. I will be fine. No matter what. I will always be your dad.

I can feel your peace though. Blood, our family line. It is here with me. Even though I can't tell you, I can feel the serenity of having you here. Having you be a part of this with me. There is undeniable comfort in that. I can't tell you, but I hope you can feel it too.

Touch. Touch is a magical thing. There are so many more statements being made with you holding me that we could say in a thousand lifetimes. You are feeding me with your soul, and I am giving you all I can. I know you must feel it too. A touch. A Connection. It is part of who we are. A bond that you and I have always shared.

Who's here? A nurse. I can tell by the way you move Heather. Adjusting. Moving. Well maybe I am not going to die yet. I really wish you wouldn't talk to each other in whispers. I can't hear whispers. Whatever you

The Scent of White

are saying, I can take it. Share it with me. I am strong enough to take it. Just tell me the truth.

Why am I suddenly so thirsty again? And I am getting tired already? It feels like I have only been up for a minute. What are you doing? Did you medicate me? Did you give me something? I can't keep my eyes open. I am so thirsty now. I really am. There is a taste. I need water to wash it away. Come on. Bring it here. Let me be at peace for a minute.

Okay, just another minute of rest. Maybe I can sleep this off. My mind doesn't need the rest. I have never been able to think this clear. I am here. But a quick rest wouldn't hurt, I guess. Just a minute. Heather stay with me. Please stay with me. I want that connection. I want your hand. That is all I want. I will see you soon sweetie. I promise I will.

Chapter 8: 1984

If imperfection is perfection, then what is imperfection? That statement couldn't have been truer in 1984. Nothing was perfect at the time. The fourth year of marriage offered some much-needed stability but being young and driven did not necessarily translate into being ready for all the road bumps of the world.

Somehow it happens that when you least expect it, and much less plan for it, the universe you the things you need. The last thing you want, maybe. But it is needed in ways that can't be defined. And those events will shake the very ground until it is solidified stronger than ever before.

When Mary walked through the bedroom door in April of 1984, Scott could see an expression he had never seen before. It was one of fear, but optimistic hope. Worry, but a deep joy. It was confusion and glee mixed in one. It was an expression that imprinted so deeply in his mind that to this day his dreams are filled with her face on that day.

The words that followed simply hung in the air; "I'm pregnant." The words that would forever change their family and the direction of their life. No matter how much planning goes into it, no matter how much

The Scent of White

time and desire a couple has, those words have an impact that is unmatched.

They both knew that eventually this day would come. It was something that they hoped for. It was part of their white picket fence dream. It was a miracle that awaited them. But in the same breath it was an unplanned adventure that they couldn't have been less prepared for. That was another moment, a moment Scott would begin to know Frank, his only son.

Neither Scott nor Mary new that it was going to be a Frank yet. But regardless, there was one thing for certain, he was loved from the moment they knew he was going to be brought into the world. Life was a flurry of dust scattered in the air as preparations were made, budgets were adjusted, and preparing for the great unknown was the only think that was on their minds.

Frank came into the world almost exactly to the day they planned for. January 10th was the day that their family unit started to become complete. There was a hole in their family that both had felt many times before. By no means was that a complaint about life, or even something that couldn't be lived without. It was more of a feeling, a need that was ingrained in both Scott and Mary. The thought of a family was powerful, and they treasured that thought.

The pregnancy was normal enough. Cravings. Growth. Sickness. Health. Glowing. Everything that a couple has been told to expect a million times before. It was the excitement of a couple in love that was turning the page to add a new chapter to the book of their lives.

The first year was a blur. Sleepless nights followed by endless days. Work made it even harder, but it gave Scott a new sense of pride to know that he was providing for the two people that he loved most. Even the pains of missing part of Franks firsts were overridden by the ability to give him a life that included love, support, and founded in stability. It was hard to know how they made it through that first year. Stress was high, sleep was little. But every trial and tribulation seemed to make the family stronger, and the bickering lead to moments of joy.

As all things do, the process of raising a child started to become routine. The illnesses that were life stopping during the first year, became just another day and part of growing up. After that first year, most nights became restful and helped them prepare for the next sunrise. Each day became another day of change and growth, but now it was expected verses the chaos of that first year.

Frank grew up as a curious kid. Not that different from any other child at that age, and Frank

The Scent of White
went through that phase of curious mischief plenty enough. Getting into slight trouble. Getting into every cabinet and drawer. Exploring. Going places that he had no business being. Climbing the tallest trees with no thought of how to get down. Shooting every single thing he could find when he got his first BB gun. Goading the neighborhood boys into following him. Frank was a leader.

No matter how much of a "boy phase" he went through, one thing stood out most. Frank was raised right. Scott and Mary made sure of that. Manners were important and saying yes sir and yes ma'am was a sign of respect to your elders. A door that you opened you held open to others. You cared for others. You always treated others with a respect that you would give yourself. It was not just about being raised right, but it was core values that meant something to the family. As much trouble as a young toddler going through adolescence could be, being raised with values kept the trouble to youthful ease.

History repeats itself; Frank broke his first bone at almost the same age as Scott. Time has a way of playing tricks on us, where the world repeats the same rights of passage from generation to generation. In the end, it may end up being a life defining moment for

Frank too, but his story was still being written. It is funny how much having a caring and supporting family helps these events play out. In times of great stress, comes great growth. Marking this growth would be a change in who each of them were, but it would be growth that would help to solidify their family even more.

Scott knew a love that he could not imagine from the first time he learned of Frank as a beating heart growing, feeding and creating. He loved Mary in a pure, true, and driven way. The way that a man should love a woman. Through respect, belief, values, and spending time everyday living for someone else as much as yourself. But there is another love, and that love comes from watching a part of you be born and grow.

When Frank first started youth T-ball it was like Scott could see himself at that age taking the first swing of the bat. Pony football, Scott could still smell the same grass and the bond of being able to play a game with friends. And if there was any doubt about it, Scott knew Frank was purely born from his cloth when they would go to the lake and he could watch the instant love for the water that they shared. Frank would have to be dragged out and a tantrum awaited every time they would have to leave. Scott would smirk every single time in private remembering how much of the same it

The Scent of White
was with his dad and himself. The long summer days at the lake were something that they all treasured.

Most teens grow away from their parents. Call it teenage angst. Call it youthful rebellion. It doesn't matter. Just like all teens Frank tested the boundaries of freedom, but something was different with him. Instead of growing away from his parents like many of his friends and the rest of the world, he seemed to grow closer. Maybe it was because Scott was understanding recognizing so much of his own youth in Frank. Or maybe it was just the product of a righteous upbringing. Either way, many of the teenage years were coupled with father and son being more of friends, with strong parental authority highlighting the relationship.

The trip through high school went in the blink of an eye. Scott could remember the first time he was able to bounce his son on his knee. The first push on a swing. And as he sat there watching Frank walk across the stage it seemed like time had not passed at all. Like it all just passed him by. Even so, looking back on the memories, each step was a treasure that he would not trade for all the days and nights before him. Those were the days they were closest. Living together, seeing each other each day and every night. Not that they grew distant, and maybe in some ways even stronger, but time together often leads to closeness. There is no greater time spent together than living in the same home.

College created a bigger question all together. While some kids just seem to have it figured out or at least have an idea of what they want to do, Frank was lost. Take a year off, join the military, just pick a university and go. It seemed like there was no right answer for him. There wasn't one thing that felt right. So, he floundered until almost graduation day. The one thing that always stuck was the values he was raised with. In the end it was the idea of putting something before himself first that appealed to him most.

There are a lot of careers where you can serve others. His choice, well Frank shipped off to boot camp that summer. He felt like he found a purpose to serve others in a way that he never could imagine. He decided to follow previous family members in joining the Army. Scott was scared to see him go, and worried to know the path that lay in front of him. Yet a bigger part of him couldn't be prouder of the choice that Frank made. Frank might have told everyone it was an excuse for four more years to decide what he wanted to do with his life, the spark of pride in his eye couldn't be denied.

The military life suited Frank from the beginning. He grew. He learned. He became a man. And

The Scent of White

for the first time in his life he started to understand who he really was. He understood all the lessons that Scott spent so much time instilling in him. Those years also had helped to define what the rest of his life would be like. While this life suited him for the time being, four years was plenty for him to be ready for a new challenge. It was time for change.

In the military, Frank's primary focus was electrical work. A far cry from the electrical work that his dad spent a career doing. It wasn't even by choice; it was where he tested high and where he fit in. There was a lot of learning that happened in those years, learning tools of the trade beyond what he thought he could retain. It made the choice for college easy. He was going to be an electrician just like his father. Go into the family business as they say. And Scott would remember getting that news too. It was a prideful moment. Even though he believed deeply Frank could do anything that he wanted, to see his son follow in his footsteps was more like a dream than he thought it would be. Just an appreciation for what his father did and wanting a similar life. A good life. A simple life.

Again, history seemed to repeat itself. Scott knew from the moment that Frank brought Lindsay home that she was going to be the one. Cheerful, happy, loyal, honest, caring. You could see so much about her from the first look. She was not perfect, no one is, but she was a perfect match for Frank, and he couldn't be happier about it. He secretly waited for the day Frank would tell him they were getting married. He knew it would happen and the day was going to be a great one.

It did happen too. A parent's intuition is almost psychic at times. To Scott, his son seemed like an extension of himself. Frank and Lindsay were married, and it is one of the only times that Scott could remember crying in years. Tears of pure joy. The expressions on their faces, and most importantly remembering those feelings from when he felt his life change after meeting Mary. Those were great days. Challenging days, but always the best. Those same days were the ones that now presented themselves to Frank. That moment is worth a thousand smiles over and over again.

While they weren't blessed with children as quickly as Scott and Mary were, he knew that they wanted it badly and eventually they would be blessed. There was a yearning to be a grandfather almost as much as one to be a father. Scott loved family and there was no doubt he would always look forward to that family growth.

The Scent of White

As Scott grew older, he realized how much he relied on Frank. Nowadays when Frank came over, there were always a few projects around the house that he would have waiting for Frank. You know, so he wouldn't get bored when he visited. But realistically they waited because he really needed a helping hand. Those projects had become common place now, and while they both played the game that it was something to do, they both knew that while Scott was extremely independent, that the extra hands were needed to get the project done in the first place.

Frank also started to become the rock of the family. While Scott would always be the patriarch, it was good to have another strong figure. When Scott eventually met his end, the family would need someone to be strong, someone to hold it together. It didn't have to be a man, often the matriarch was the stronger one. But in this family Scott was the strong one, the leader. Frank was quickly filling that role. It was good. It was handing the baton to the next generation and while it is completely superficial, in many ways it felt like it was the changing of the guard.

Frank was created unexpectedly, brought up with unconditional love, and developed into being a man that everyone could be proud of. A father and son will always share a bond that is special and from that bond generational traits will be passed down through the years. That love that was born in January was one that made an impact on the world that day.

Scott knew that a part of his life was forever altered. His first born. His only son. Looking back on each step of his life, he knew it would be empty if Frank had not been a part of it. There was a longing in that light that was the spark. A ray of light that added to the shine of his life well lived. When you look back at the dash between the years of your life, that dash is filled with beams that exclude what life really was about, and you could guarantee that Frank would always be a shining light in that dash.

The Scent of White
Chapter 9: dying, part 5

I am dying. Everything hurts. My whole body. No, it is more than that. Even my soul hurts. I can feel it everywhere. I can feel it inside. I am dying.

I won't give up the fight, fight the good fight as they say. I am a fighter, and I will give it my all. Yet, I have to accept that this might be the end, the real end. Not the beginning of the end, not the middle of the end, but the real end of everything. Then again, maybe it is the beginning. The next step in a life eternal.

This whole time I have been trying to figure out what is going on. Place it all together. There has been no time to gain acceptance, only time to deal with the here and now. Family was a great distraction. I needed that. I needed to feel that love. I needed to understand I am not alone. I can't imagine those that go through this alone. I am so thankful for those caring for me.

Every time I wake up here is the same. Take Stock. Remember. Try and comprehend. Figure out what is new, and what is the same. Now though I need to take a minute to give myself time to accept what is happening, not just deal with it. I need to do it for the others too. Give them closure. Close this chapter myself. Move on.

So, what do I know? It was a beautiful night. The dog was restless. I was restless. So, a walk it was. I remember bits and pieces, but I can't remember where I was at. Did I make it home? Did Mary have to see me fall? God, I hope she was spared from that. But that was it. That was my moment. My life was forever changed again. I had a stroke. Nothing will ever be the same.

Let's see, after that I woke up here. I am incapable of the simplest task, an invalid. I can't even get up to pour a glass of water. I am still so thirsty. It took a long time. Days? Hours? Weeks? Months? Time really has no meaning anymore. It is hard to understand. Comatose. Not medically induced, well aside from whatever drugs are pumping into me through all these tubes and machines. At least my mind is clear. I know why I am here.

I have spent my entire life preaching to the kids that you need to be open to change in order to grow. Well here I am, open to change, but I am not changing. I am not getting better. I haven't progressed. There has been a whole team of doctors running around taking care of me, poking me, testing me. Now it is a nurse here and there and the random required stop of the doctor to see if there is anything that changed. I am not changing. My whole life has been about growth,

The Scent of White

development, and change. Now I am just sitting here in my own personal purgatory. That is where I am now.

My family is with me though. They are my support. Their love has been what has kept me going. Well that and a cocktail of drugs that I am sure I am on right now. I need to be here for them. At least until I can see the closure in their eyes. That will be the time I know I can move on. That is so dark, but there is peace in it too. I need that. I need to know that when I leave this place, they are going to be good. That is important.

I am dying. I can learn to accept it. Aside from a miracle, that is where I am. I still have faith. I have hope. However, without that miracle, no growth is the moment we die. Is this what acceptance looks like? Cliché I know, but from the day that we are born we start dying. But we still get every single day to live, and that is a gift. No matter how well I understand that, is it not just as important to understand that there is no guarantee of tomorrow either?

So here I am. Dying. What is next? If you are going to accept that you are dying, then you must accept the last tomorrow is near. Then what, do I become worm food? Is there a heaven? A hell? If I accepted my death, I need to accept this too.

I have never been a religious man. Agnostic. That is the term society uses. There is a higher level of being. I can feel that. Every precious sun set, that feeling you get deep inside when you are in the middle of nature. A peace that overcomes your entire being when you are closer to the mother of all, earth. That is God. I just never could figure out how the law of man taught in a church was somehow greater than the natural order of things.

I like to think I go and become a part of that nature. Not in rebirth but in being a part of that energy that surrounds us. That is heaven if you will. I have always liked the thought that regardless if my soul moves on and knows who and what, that my spirit and soul will continue on forever found in the energy that surrounds us in the world. That is what is next for me, I think. If I can accept my death, I can accept my being moving on too. At the purest form, even if it is just being planted in the ground, I will become part of something so much bigger than me. My essence will live beyond this shell.

Accepting my death, accepting that I am dying, I can rest at peace. Then this damn thirst will go away finally. I will find contentment and fulfillment in the life I have lived by realizing and rationalizing my death.

The Scent of White

Maybe. But for right now this thirst is all I am. Water is what I have needed and what I will continue to need.

For once I am not tired. I am not exhausted. A little peace of mind can go a long way now. I want my family. I want them to look into the window of my soul through my eyes. I want them to see the peace that is in there. I want to give them peace. Peace and love. Let them know it will be ok. I will be ok. I will always be a part of them, surrounding them.

Chapter 10: 2012

Retirement. That word sounds like being put out to pasture. Scott hated that word but loved the idea of freedom. So much of an adult life is spent looking for the next step. The next car, the bigger house, the next goal or ambition that we feel driven to work toward. And for the vast majority, one of those steps it is looking forward to retirement.

That is not to say Scott, like the majority of the world, didn't take the time to stop and enjoy the little things. He loved watching his kids grow. Enjoyed each end of day with Mary. It was loads of fun planning vacations and events with the family. All of those were amazing experiences that he wouldn't trade for the world. Retirement symbolized freedom. Financial freedom. Time that doesn't need to be spent toiling away. That was alluring to him. He would have all the time in the day to live the life he had always wanted to live.

He didn't have a clue what the life he wanted to live looked like, but he was ready to figure it out. Over the years of building a family and working and hustling to make sure that his family was provided for, a lot of his personal joys and hobbies had to take a back seat. Now he didn't even know where to start. That is a big part of why he hated the word retirement. It was a step

The Scent of White

to constantly look forward to, but now that he was there, he had no plan. He couldn't figure out why it felt like the end of a big part of his life at the same time it felt like the beginning of a new adventure. It was the most basic example of the duality of man.

Over the years Scott had always been an electrician of some sort. He had worked for companies, worked independently when the markets had fallen, taken a few jobs on the side, but for the last 18 years he had gone to work every day at the local mill. It was as job that just seemed to fit him. He was allowed some independence. He could work in ways that seemed to make a difference. He had a small team to work with. And at the end of the day he was always able to go home to his family. That is what made it the best for him. He loved that he had a schedule that fit with family life. He was a family man after all. But that was all over now.

What made him do it? Why 2012? Heather was just getting ready to graduate high school. Frank was well on his own now and doing well in the military. There were still things to do, and family to raise. Unfortunately for Scott it came down to his health. Over the past few years he had been noticing that his hands were stiffer than normal, some of the intricate operations he couldn't handle like he did in the past. He knew the time was coming. There were still side jobs he could do and make a few bucks, but the end was coming quicker than what he wanted.

The final straw came when John, the mill foreman called him into the shop office. Everyone had a good idea of the situation he was facing. No one would force him out, he had a job as long as he wanted it. The goal was to hit his full retirement package and for that he needed to be able to work for exactly 394 more days. The countdown was on. There was a little shock in the air and a little bit of wariness as he made his way up to the office that day.

The news that was to come would alter the path Scott thought he was on for the rest of his life. John had called him in for what he could only assume was a performance and retirement talk. It has been coming for quite a while. He just wasn't ready yet, and he couldn't give up the money he would be losing retiring early. It was a dilemma. The news John had to offer was much better than that. The company was buying out his last year to retirement. He was going to be allowed to retire early, still be a consultant on big projects for the mill and receive his entire compensation package. Now it was just a matter of setting a date.

The Scent of White

August 15th was that date for Scott. That would give him plenty of time not to interfere with his daughter's graduation, have a great summer with family, and be able to retire within a few months. It was all roses as they say.

That summer went by like lightening. There was absolutely no slowing down it seemed. The days were all in preparation, the next great adventure. All his affairs needed to be in order. Money had to be saved and managed. Financial advisers were contacted. Heather needed to be ready for college. There was never a free minute. All the great summer plans that were made were put on temporary hold or thought about twice before they proceeded. It was all part of what needed to be done. Scott preferred to be busy rather than spend his time in a whirlwind of doing nothing.

When August 14th came, the real panic set in. The next day was going to be a busy. Work would probably be more of a grand sendoff than a normal workday, and there would be time needed to clear out his desk. That wouldn't be hard. He had been working for so many years he had gotten good at only keeping around the essentials. Besides, it was not like it was going to be his last time in the mill. After the workday, a nice dinner with the family would follow. Then the retirement party. Everything was spinning in high gear.

Looking at it though clearer eyes, the panic had nothing to do with the last day of work, the panic came from knowing it was the end. The next day was when his new life would begin. Everything was going to be different. His mornings would be free, opposed to the routine he developed over all his working career. His purpose during the workweek was gone. He was going to be a free man now, but a free man with no plans, and no idea of what he would do. What was retirement supposed to bring? That is where the panic began. The more Scott thought about it, the more it scared him.

Those first few days of retirement felt like a weekend. That is pretty much what it was comparable too. Just another weekend. Then the first week. That was pretty much like a vacation, or maybe even a long weekend. Not really that much different at all. Then came the first month. That wasn't so bad either. There were a lot of projects that had been put off because of lack of time or lack of motivation, but now there was plenty of time and nothing else on his list. It felt great to get those accomplishments taken care of and get his little space caught up.

Month two. Now retirement was getting real. The weather had started to turn so not every day could

The Scent of White

be spent outdoors. The projects that had been put off were now somehow done. The extra little things that took up the day seemed to come to a halt. Now came the big question, what now? Mary was a huge help. She always had something up her sleeve and Scott was happy to lend a hand. It was always a pleasure to be a part of her life in any way that he could. Ultimately those events were limited as well. The dye was cast, he was going to have to find himself again.

There are many different journeys that can lead to self-awareness and self-discovery. Those journeys can show us who we are, our goals and dreams, or even the passions we really enjoy. The journey can be daunting and bigger than all imagination, but Scott was motivated with nothing to lose. That combination makes for eye-opening drive. He was about to find a part of his live that had never been dreamed of before.

Scott's journey started with trying out everything that he remembered liking in years past, but had slipped away from him. Over the winter months he tried woodworking again. It was fun, but not his passion. Metal work? Not his thing anymore. He used to like tinkering with small motors, but that really didn't seem to hit the spot either. All winter went like this. New idea, it passed the time, but not what he was looking for. It continued into the spring. Another idea, just not the right fit. It made the winter and spring months feel even longer than they were. The family time was his saving grace, and the little projects, events, and time with his dog were great saviors when it came to some form of responsibilities, but there was something missing.

The lightning bolt came in late spring. Everything became obvious. All the best days he could remember were spent the same way. The time with family that brought the biggest smiles were always at the same place. There was only one place where he had truly felt at peace, a sense of contentment and fulfillment. By the water.

It seemed so simple after that moment. All of the best parts of his life seemed to revolve around the lake and time spent there with family. They would boat. He would fish. They would swim. He would explore. There were a million adventures to be had on and around the water. The idea was to turn that special place into much more. By mid-May his mind was made up. He would spend his summer and probably every season beyond by the lake. Maybe even move out to a lake side house if Mary was ready for a move and everything went as planned.

The Scent of White

That summer was one of the best of Scott's life. He would spend long leisurely days fishing and exploring all the lakeside areas within driving distance. Mary would often be his fishing partner. On the weekends, it wasn't uncommon for the kids to come to the lake and spend it with the family. On the side, he had been meeting with the local bank and a realtor to see what the possibilities were to put in a purchase offer on a small house that he had spent the summer eyeing up. It would be emotionally hard to sell the family home. Where a family was raised, where he and his sweet Mary had so many firsts, but at the same time this was where they were mean to be. It symbolized a lot of who they had become as a family. It would also give them a special spot for many years to come.

Contentment and fulfillment. Two words that are so often overlooked when it comes to the meaning of life. Everyone tells you the same thing. Be happy. Do what makes you happy. Happiness is a virtue of life. So much time is spent chasing happiness value is taken away from the simple pleasures in living a good life. Instead Scott had spent his life with purpose, the search for contentment and fulfillment. He felt when you are content with yourself and your life, then your experiences would be full. Then by filling your life with what is important, happiness is the byproduct. That doesn't mean every minute will be happy, nor should it be. Instead there was a lack of negativity and a feeling that the days were going to be good whether he found elusive happiness.

By the second year of retirement Scott and Mary were moving. They had found the perfect small house on a nearby lake. It wasn't the first one that Scott had eyed up. That was just too soon, it didn't fit. But when this house came along, the fit was no question. They would have to downsize a bit, but that is what couples did at their age. They didn't need all the space or all the material things. Far from minimalists, just a nice mix of having most of what you want and all of what you need.

They would grow there. Their grandchildren would always have a fun, safe place to play. Their family would have peace when they visited. It was a perfect situation. The community was friendly. He and Mary had already spent so much time on the water, the move felt more like they were moving to an old neighborhood rather than starting completely new. There was a good vibe all around their future and the new home.

Retirement had found a purpose in Scott. It wasn't all fishing and ice fishing or tooling around the lake. There were still projects to get done at home. There were still peaceful evenings in. Even the

The Scent of White

mundane parts had a way of becoming important moments. The things that mean something. The quiet times spent just being, either alone or with the person that has spent their life with you. Those are the times to be cherished. Scott had found an outlet for his passion on top of those times. Experiences that would serve to make his life more than complete. It was a mixture that made life worth living and living to the fullest.

For the next 7 years this was going to be retirement for Scott. These were the years that would make memories for not just he and Mary, but for the entire family. There could be a hundred scrapbooks dedicated to these years. They would be filled with fall colors, spring blooms, storms, sunrises, sunsets, family, friends, and all the good parts of life. There were neighbors that had turned more into family. There were constant adventures. Explorations of all the land, nature and community had to offer.

Scott had even found himself breaking out of his routine life. He was volunteering more in the community. He was taking on challenges and organizing events. He spent more time finding solace in the people that surrounded him every day. Retirement had changed from being put out to pasture into a purposeful being. It was a passion that he had never known in his life. He had known love. He had known work. He had known all the parts of life that comes with familiarity to day to day living. But he had never felt the fire and the drive that he did by that water and the experienced which were gleaned from it.

There was a rhythm there too. A schedule that seemed to come from its own doing. Morning coffee was made the same way at nearly the same time. The mail would come. The days would pass with a steady beat that had a beauty in its own way. Variation would encompass each day, but they were all far from losing the rhythm found there. That rhythm is what drove them all forward. The end of each day came the same. His dog would get antsy knowing what was to come. Scott would almost feel a restlessness himself. The end of the day was always saying hi to the neighbors that were out. Taking in the sights that magically seemed to change each day just for them. They would go for a walk.

The Scent of White
Chapter 11: Dying part 6

Oh god everything hurts more now. I can't tell if this is dying or if I just have been in the same damn position for too long. I am staying awake longer now. I am not quite as tired, that is progress. But every muscle. Ouch. Every damn one hurts. Who knew that dying would hurt so much, my body must be shutting down.

Am I alone? It is weird. Even though I know that I am awake, my eyes won't focus right away. Is it the drugs? Are my eyes partially paralyzed too? What is this? Where is my focus. Come on focus!

There we go. It's turning white again. White is good. The sterile walls are coming back. White is always what happens before light. It WILL come back. It has to. More and more, it is coming into view. There is someone here. There are two people.

Before I can even focus, I can tell that one is a nurse. So busy. Not nearly as busy as before, but always moving. I wonder if they keep moving so they don't have to see death. Keeping busy is probably a pretty good distraction from letting yourself feel. I am ecstatic that they can do this job, I know that I never could. I get attached to people to easy.

Who else is here? Is it weird that I can feel their presence even before I can see them? I can tell by that huge hulking frame. It's Frank. Yes. That is my boy. He is here for me. He is always here for me. I feel sorry for him sometimes. He has had to take on so much. Yea, he is the strong one. He has become the rock of the family even if he doesn't know it yet. At the same time, it has to weigh heavily on a young man that is living his own life with his own family. Everyone probably goes through that at some point, another rite of passage into adulthood responsibilities. It just doesn't seem fair to me. Oh god I hurt.

Look at me Frank. Come on look at me. See into my eyes. You can see me. You can see I am here with you. Everyone that has came in so far has only been able to see my shell. They can't see into my soul, see the real me. Will you be the one?

"Hi Dad" Those are the sweetest words I could ever imagine hearing. I don't know if I am crying, but I can feel that swell of emotion on the inside ready to burst out. That is all I needed to hear from him. I can hear him talking, but I can't even fully focus on his words. What I can focus on is his eyes. I can see all the sadness there. The tears that are literally formed at the corners of his eyes. The ones that want to flow like rivers, but he will never let them out.

The Scent of White

Don't look away Frank. I know the tears are hard to hold back. I have been there bud. I have. I know it isn't fun to be strong. You can cry. But I know, you will always choose the side of showing strength instead. Not for yourself. Not because of pride. You are holding the tears back for me. For your mom. For your sister. Even the strongest men cry too Frank, I wish I would have told you that more.

I know people think you won't cry because you are a man. That's not true. You are humble. You are not prideful. You won't cry because you are the rock. You are strong because you need to be strong. You have learned so much. You know what it means to really take care of others.

I know Frank. I know you don't want me to go. I know how much you need me. Truth is you haven't needed me for years. Regardless, it is a guilty pleasure of mine to have you still come to me. I know it isn't need. It is wanting. We all want to be together. We are family. Family is strong. And Frank I am so proud of you.

If I could choose to tell you one thing right at this moment, that would be it. I am proud of who you are. I hear your words. I would love to listen to every single one. Instead, all I can think is the pride I feel as I look at all you are. You are here. You are comforting me. That is beautiful. However, I would much rather tell you those words.

You are me. You have always been a part of me. You are one of the purest souls and you are a caretaker. The one value I have cherished passing on more than all the others has been how you treat others. Even with all the words you are speaking, you don't need to take care of me. Let me bring you peace through that. I want for my children to be free. Not of me, but of the pain I can see in your eyes. My gift to you Frank, let it be to be free of taking care of me.

I am tired now. I want you stay with me son. I need all my family, but right now just let it be us. Sit with me. You don't need to talk. Hold my arm. Rest with me. Your touch that is what I need. I enjoy your touch. It is a connection.

What I don't understand is how each time I am with one of you, my thirst feels a little more quenched. How can a physical need be filled by an emotional one? That is mind boggling. No matter how baffling, it is true.

I have been up for a long time. It's ok that I am tired. I know it is. I can nap. I need a nap. There is more to come. More to my story. I know there is. A quick recharge. Just a litt….

The Scent of White
Chapter 12: 1987

Simple blessings can make your life complete, and the blessing of a child is one of the greatest. Another child then must be considered a gift from the heavens themselves. While Frank had been a bit of a surprise for Scott, Heather had been just what he and Mary had been waiting for. From the moment they were granted this gift, pure joy had filled the home.

By the summer of 1986 Frank had grown up quite a bit, fully embracing the toddler stage. He was running around and starting to become more and more capable every day. It was joyful to watch him grow like that. The feeling that only bringing a child into the world can bring. It was that feeling of fulfillment that led Scott and Mary to start thinking that they might want to grow the family a little more.

Frank might have been a bit of a surprise, but both knew it was a blessing. They knew how hard it could be as they watched several of their friends try for a child or another child. It was a time to stay humble while they tried. They knew it might not happen. However, it didn't take long before they needed to plan for Heather. They started their journey in June, and by September they were pulling out the baby supplies for the next bundle of joy.

Scott had to admit the next 10 months were some of the toughest in his life. He watched pain and suffering in a way that he never knew he could feel. Mary was a trooper, this pregnancy hit her hard to the point where she was on bedrest for several weeks as Heather grew. But through the entire process the wonder and the radiant glow never left her beautiful face. The family was going to be complete, and when Heather entered this world on July 14th, 1987 the feeling of being complete never left their family or Scott again.

Heather was a great baby from the start. While Frank had kept them on their toes, Heather had an inner peace in her soul that made her so different than what they had come to know about raising a child. She took to sleeping through the night almost immediately. She never seemed to make a fuss. There was a light in her eyes that seemed to sparkle and shine and only grew when she took in something new. Scott could watch her for hours as she sat there in pure amazement seeing how she experienced the world.

There was a delicacy to her as well. There was strength there too, but the delicacy brought out the softness in her that nurtured other living things, that made you feel how kind a heart could be. And a heart of gold was something not lost on her. From an early age

The Scent of White
Scott had called her his sunflower. Bright, beautiful, and always reaching for the things that were warm and shiny above.

A favorite memory always would come to mind when she was six years old and just learning to ride a two-wheeler by herself. He had been helping her for a few days and no matter how much practice, it never worked out just right. He could see a sad determination in her eyes, only sad from the effort not being rewarded. The determination was pure and driven by a motivation that only a child could have after countless near successes. The moment it finally clicked was amazing. It was up and down the street, around the block. Testing out all the new freedom that comes with taking your bike into independence. When she fell off, it was him that she came running to, her delicacy on full display. But with a simple hug and a kiss, all the strength she possessed came rushing back in a way that could be seen through the darkest shroud.

Scott had lost count of how many "injured" or "stray" animals she would bring home. There were nights of nursing a baby squirrel back to health or building a temporary habitat for a random salamander that she would find in the wood pile out back. One summer keeping a baby turtle as a pet she found at the lake. Caring for it and feeding it all summer long until the fall hit and releasing it back into the wild to find its own family. She was a nurturer by nature and his appreciation for that side of her was remarkable. Regardless if she tried to make their home look like a zoo from time to time it was a quality that endured in her.

It was her nature that helped her grow into a tender, strong force in the family. Scott may have been the great protector, and Mary the caregiver, sometimes you had to question where they would be without Heather taking them all to places they could have never gone alone.

Even when the teenage years hit and so many young girls find it the time to test their parents, especially their mothers, Heather never did. She valued her time with family. She might be called an old soul by some, but for her, she only focused on the things which held true value.

Scott's memories sometimes would trick him into thinking of the perfection of those years. As with all families, there were good times and hard times. There were fights. There were tears. There were times that Scott and Mary thought Frank and Heather would punch each other out. But all those times combined

The Scent of White
were such a small speck in the existence and time that made up such a bright life.

It was in the way it presented to the world as well. Scott was adamant that she would not date until she was 16. He wanted her to have boys that were friends and to connect with everyone that she met, but he was worried for her. Worried about boys. Worried about what his beautiful girl would encounter as she grew, and the boys took notice. He had no reason to worry. Her friends may have started to be boy crazy, but Heather always wanted something different.

Even with all his ideology, there was no denying an adolescent girl and her mother when they were on the same side. He knew his views were old fashioned, and probably out of favor, but he was going to protect his little girl with all he had. So, when at 14 she was asked to a school dance by a boy, there was no fight in him to deny the women he loved. It was innocent and completely safe, but for the first time he had to trust all the years of raising her and pray all the lessons were the right ones.

With her mother's insistence, it would be set. That was to be the start of her first real boyfriend, Tim or Tom or something like that. It is funny, what seemed like a big deal then he couldn't even remember the kids name a few years later. He watched with the eye of a hawk as their relationship bloomed. At least to the extent that a high school freshman's relationship can bloom. She didn't sneak out. She didn't seem to try and hide away to be with him alone. As odd as it seemed, even at 14 and 15 you could see her mind judging and evaluating where the relationship could go. It was as though she was guided to create something for herself that was the same as the relationship she saw growing up. She was creating a world for herself that she could take pride in and led her to accomplishments of the things she wanted in life.

That day when Scott found Heather in tears and broken more than he ever had seen, it tore his heart into pieces. He never did find out the reason that Heather's first boyfriend broke up with her, and he never really cared. What drove the rage and sadness in him was seeing what it did to his girl. All those emotions lead to one of the happiest memories that he could create. It wasn't original. It was corny. It was strait out of the worst romance movie sold on the shelf. But that night he stayed up late with her and watched terrible movies. He brought her ice cream. He stayed with her and just reminded her how much love she deserved and how she should be treated. Even the look on Mary's face that night let him know he did something right.

The Scent of White

When it was time for college, Heather had dreams. At first, they thought it might be nursing school, and then maybe veterinary medicine. She was a whirlwind of ideas, but they always came back to professions where she could serve others. The nurturer in her character had come out full force. Finally, she settled in a psychology. Helping people was always going to be who she was and being able to listen to someone could not have been a better fit.

Those years were tough. Not for Heather, she was succeeding with flying colors. It was the first time that Scott and Mary became empty nesters. It was although there was a divide in the world that a bridge had yet to be built across, so on that day that Heather graduated and decided to look for work, or maybe even open her own practice back in her home town, it brought contentment to Scott. Independent, but together. Each family member would be close, and they would celebrate each other's independence and allow it to make the entire family strong.

She did find work fairly quickly. It started off working for one of the juvenile homes and working with youth. Quickly she moved up and started working for the state as a mental health provider for youth throughout the county. It suited her. Being able to work so closely with children was something that she loved more than anything else she did. It only troubled her to be constrained by policy and regulation to not be able to help more. So when she came to Scott and Mary for a loan to start her own practice, right before her thirtieth birthday, they knew it would be a success on many more levels than financially.

Her practice grew quickly. She was helping members of the community, developing alternative therapies, and seeing her successes in the community. She could watch her clients grow and blossom. While she loved specializing in the youth, she found a quiet bliss in being able to work with her peers and seeing the gratitude, and more importantly the changes that she could be a part of in each life she touched. A Midas touch if there ever was one.

Her soul, her passion did have drawbacks. She always saw the best in others and was willing to let go of parts of herself to accommodate all the good that she could see even when others couldn't. She would go out of the way to help, even if her help wasn't appreciated. She would give of herself in order to build others around her into the potential she could see. It was her nature, and her downfall with so many. You could see the hurt and frustration when she couldn't touch someone, but that same drive and determination

The Scent of White
that she possessed learning to ride a bike never faded away like it did for so many of us, instead it seemed to make the fire burn even hotter inside of her.

There was no place this was more apparent than in her search for that person to build her own family. Heather was a beautiful girl on all accounts. She had plenty of young mean fawning over her and trying to find a place in her shine. She had dated through college and had found a couple long term relationships. Even after college there were a few different men that she would bring home to meet the family, but they never seemed to stick.

Scott had taken a liking to Ryan. It wasn't one of her longer relationships, but Scott could see the look in Ryan's eye, and it reminded him of the way that he looked at Mary. It was the same look he held to this day. Puppy love and lust have their own look. The look Scott had briefly saw was one of a man that was going to count his blessings and treat this woman like a queen. His queen for as long as she would have him. He cherished that look. But Ryan wasn't to last. Heather needed a challenge in her life. Not intellectually, she wanted to challenge of bringing out the potential in her partner.

She dated men that cheated. She dated men that didn't appreciate all the effort she put into them. She dated men that wanted her as a trophy. She dated men that had a past. It wasn't to get back at her parents. It wasn't because she didn't love herself. It was all because she saw sunshine in the clouds and thought there was a way to make the ray of sunshine poke through to shine brighter than the rest. It just hadn't occurred to her yet that no matter how bright and warm the sunbeam could be, it wouldn't break through unless it wanted to be seen.

Scott had no idea if maybe there was a right way or a wrong way to build a relationship. The experience he and Mary had was theirs, and not hers. He had no idea if it would work out for her and she would find the potential she was looking for. All he knew is that one of the things that tore him up inside was seeing how much she wanted a family and how much she wanted to have all good that she had been privy to for herself. His one solace is that as she grew, wisdom was taking hold. The potential she looked for now wasn't potential in what could come, but rather the potential in a beam that was already lit and could only become brighter.

With age comes wisdom, but our soul, our driving light, always stays the same. Heather was taking

The Scent of White

on the role she was born to play. While the project list got longer for Frank because Scott needed him more, he needed Heather just as much. Her visits now always consisted of making sure everything around the house was cared for. Clean, tidy, and that the family plans were right on track. Nothing was forgotten. Mary was still the matriarch, but as we age, we start to rely on our family for help. Even if it isn't needed, it is appreciated.

Heather's growing family role was solidifying. The caretaker of the family. Frank may be the one to hold everyone together, but it would no doubt be Heather that made sure everyone was taken care of. Her ability to rise above herself and make sure those around her were taken care of first was apparent. It was inspiring to watch her give the fertilizer needed for each family member to grow into all they could be. And like Frank, she was being passed the torch from Mary and carrying it to new heights. Grounded in the roots of what had come before her.

Heather had taught him so much. She had brought out emotion and taught him the tenderness of a love for a child. She had made him stop to appreciate the world and take a second look. The sparkle in her eye led to some discoveries that cannot be comprehended but only felt. That made him a complete man. His puzzle was complete by itself, but each new member of his family added pieces to his puzzle that changed the shape. It made his puzzle grow. While his puzzle was complete independently, if you took a part out now it would forever have a missing piece that could not be replaced. Heather was and would always be the last piece to his puzzle.

The Scent of White
Chapter 13: Dying, part 7

What's left for me? Routine. That seems to be what this has become, right? I wake up, maybe a little easier each time, realize my surroundings, get tired, fall back asleep. It is routine now. Nothing has changed. Damn it. Nothing has changed.

There is peace in routine. It was has always driven me. Ah this room. The beeping. That is all there is. It might routine, but it is still maddening as all hell. Where is my family? Where is anybody? The nurses are not as frequent. No doctors. Nobody. Alone. Is that all there is now, alone? Loneliness? That is self-pity.

Stop it. I can't allow myself more than a minute of that. I must move past those thoughts. To what? I have no idea. I have to move forward. Move forward to something. Speaking of movement... Who is that? I can feel someone coming. Frank? Heather? Why can't I turn my head yet? Just a little further. I can feel you there, I can sense you, but I can't see you yet. Come into my vision. Come and see me.

Well that can't be good. I know that collar. The good reverend is here. I can't believe a reverend came for me. I have not been the best church going man. Hell, I don't even know what I believe anymore. I believe in something. There is something greater than me, I can feel that. But I sure can't define it. I don't know if I am more shocked that he came or that it must be time for last rites. There is something there though. He is looking at me. No that isn't it. He isn't looking at me. He sees me. The real me.

Maybe dealing with death every day has given him a perspective others don't obtain. Maybe he really is closer to the afterlife than the rest of us. I don't know what it is, but when he is looking at me, I know he isn't seeing the shell of a man that is in front of him. He is looking through that. He is looking at me. He is communicating with me.

"I know this is hard."

You are damn right this is hard. This isn't hard, this is impossible. It is an impossible situation at an impossible time. It is nothing. It is everything. It is all rolled into one.

"I know that you can understand me, I know your soul."

But you don't know me at all. You don't know who I was. You don't know who I am. What does that mean you know my soul? I don't even know if I can tell my soul apart from the rest of me. Sure, I have felt it. Soulful feelings I can't explain. I know there is more to

The Scent of White

me than what you see, but how can you know anything?

"You are fighting a good fight my son. I am here with you."

Do I want you here? It is peaceful. You are the first one to really see me. But how can a complete stranger see me? Should you be here? What if we don't believe in the same thing? Can you see through that too? There are so many questions. Why are your words the ones that are piercing this fog more than the others? That doesn't make sense to me. My beliefs are my own and I highly doubt we would see eye to eye on them, but you are offering me peace. How rare is it to find love and peace in a stranger?

"I am not here to preach to you if that is what you are thinking. Your family has not asked for last rites, nor do I think it is that time. I am only here to offer you the comfort I offer all the travelers of this world."

Well that clears that up. But does it? I don't really know what he means. But I do feel the comfort in his experience, his wisdom. A traveler of this earth, that is what I have been. For how much longer, well I guess that is the question no one has an answer too. I don't feel fear though. I like this man's presence here. Clarity.

I don't really know what that is like, but I seem to feel it at the moment. It all is ok. Even if I don't know what all of it is.

"Let us take a moment. I will pray for you. You can pray if you like."

What would I pray for? Who would I pray too? The Christian God of my youth? The force of something greater that I feel every time I am alone in nature. What does that look like? Forgive me reverend. I don't know if I can, I don't know what that would look like. All I know is what I feel. So no, I don't think I will pray, but I will feel. I will let myself slip off into peace. I will feel that thing that is greater than I am. I will let myself be found on the water. In the one place that I can always feel what you seem to see so definitely and clearly. There I will feel it. I can feel the warmth of that thought. I am going to close my eyes and fade into that peace.

I am tired. I have visions of my place in this world. My place on and in the water. My place. My feeling. That will carry me to rest.

The Scent of White
Chapter 14: 2018

Growing old sucks. Everyone seems to have the same opinion. Growing old is the worst thing that can happen to us. Our wisdom increases. Our abilities decrease. Our mind becomes clearer and thoughts are like lightening. The body becomes less strong and tired. Our health becomes a primary concern as things start to weaken and shut down. Our passion and desires never fade. It is the law of inverse relationships spelt out in real life step by step.

The dirty little secret that no one can admit with a hubris of ego is that growing old doesn't suck. Ask anyone who had a life that was cut too short, taken too soon. They will tell you in a resounding shout. Growing old is a privilege and one that should never be taken lightly. Growing old is a gift that must be cherished and savored through each painful step and each joyous experience.

Scott was seeing with more clarity everyday how much grow and age he was allowed compared to others. Sixty years old seems young to most adults, and it seems ancient to most kids. It is unique that with age comes the perspective to see what is happening. The world seems to shift. Things that were once important, don't seem quite as big. Simple things gain more traction and priority. The world takes a breath with you instead of racing by.

Scott first noticed this when after 4 years of retirement he could feel his days slipping by more slowly and with careful planning. At one point in his life, taking a day out on the lake meant that he would have to work harder to get all the chores done and keep his world running like a well-oiled machine. Now taking a day on the lake was a simple pleasure, those other chores would get done eventually or maybe they wouldn't. The importance came from taking that time out, to feel calm, peaceful, and surrounded by the people who mean the most. The rest wasn't as important. Truthfully, not important at all.

He had found himself realizing all those years of keeping his garage and workspace meticulously clean was a cycle of repetition as it became dirty again. It was not about being slovenly, but a few more specks of sawdust didn't really matter. The world kept turning regardless of how much time he spent cleaning, it was another moment in time.

Who could have ever known that the health we ignored so much as children would come for us with a vengeance? In his twenties and thirties Scott could not remember ever going to the doctor. Maybe there was a virus that sent him once or twice. He remembered

The Scent of White

bringing the kids there. He could honestly never remember a time that he went himself. There was no need. Colds would come and go. Being sick was never any fun, but it would pass with mild discomfort. It was all just a part of life.

Somewhere around forty that all started to change. All of a sudden things would pop up that seemed to have no explanation. A shooting pain in the shoulder. Heartburn that wouldn't go away. Random ailments that would come and go. Things were happening now that he didn't have an explanation for and were persistent enough that it would warrant a trip to the doctor's office to get checked out.

Were these trips to the doctor now caused because he really had more things happening to his body or was it because his mind started to realize the invincibility of youth was fading? Regardless, health had become a priority. There was not a good answer in his mind for these ailments. Maybe it was a little of both. His health mattered, if not for himself, to be there for the people and experiences that mattered. Each day as his body grew older and more tired, it was apparent he needed to take care.

And the soreness. No one mentioned that. Scott had always kept himself in pretty good shape. Going to the gym was not a daily habit, but it was a part of his life. Now after a long day's work he would wake up sore and need to stretch before hopping out of bed. That was new. There were so many little things that would leave him a little stiff and sore now. Using muscles a little different. Being active for more than a few minutes. All of it would cause a chain reaction of physical events that he had never considered before.

Growing old also brought along the companion of death. Death is a familiarity that we are born with. Grandparents died. Parents died. Scott had seen death throughout his life, but there is a difference. When friends and classmates start dying you take notice. There had been a few people about the same age that died over the years. Accidents and diseases that happen which end a life much too young. So often that is written off in our minds. Scott knew that was part of the world as much as everyone else did.

In the last few years death had taken on a different meaning. "Natural Causes" started to show up in the obituaries. His friend Mark had a massive heart attack at 55 years old and never recovered. Susan was a family friend, she died of complications from diabetes at 62. Their neighbor Joe passed away at 59, no one really knew the cause, but it was a natural death.

The Scent of White

Then there was that bastard cancer. So many friends and family seemed to be fighting it all at once. Some won the battle for now, and others did not. But does anyone ever really win? Years of life taken away from radiation and chemotherapy. The same medicines that would help, could and would eventually kill. It was a cruel joke that was played. They fought the good fight, but the result always seemed to be the same, it was a battle that showed no signs of relief from the pages of aging.

There are so many negative aspects of aging and Scott had spent a lot of time when he first retired experiencing and seeing that perspective. In reality, those thoughts started long before retirement. Now he had the time to really think about it, and without the other daily distractions. His eyes were not what they used to be and that bugged him. His strength would fade away, and he relied on Frank more. It all seemed like a contradiction compared to the daily wisdom he gained. So much clarity with so much less ability.

As the old adage says, with age comes wisdom. It didn't happen overnight, and it seldom does. Scott didn't notice it right away either. It happened as some of the best things do. He started to appreciate the soreness in his body as the result of being able to still complete projects and enjoy his time. Those deaths around him started to give Scott gratitude for still being alive. It was a slow change, but as the winds shift over the sea, the priorities of our lives have a way of blowing in different directions as well.

Scott had noticed his mind had become like a lightning bolt with ideas and thoughts. No matter how much life slowed down, it was a clarity of thought that he hadn't experienced before. By no means was it a stroke of genius or some unexplained beautiful mind. It was the combination of time and wisdom colliding. When life slowed down there were less distractions. With less distractions came focus. And with focus came clarity.

Some days he could afford to just sit and think. That led to ideas. Sometimes those ideas Mary wasn't quite as thrilled about, but ideas none the less. His project list was growing. He had always battled with diseases and pests in his garden. It seemed like an ongoing battle. But last summer after a serious thinking session he designed and built a hydroponic raised bed system that took half the care and created a healthier growing plant. That backyard gazebo that always seemed like too much work to learn how to build, became a plan with follow through. It was time to sit and contemplate.

The Scent of White

The ideas weren't all projects. They were concepts. Thoughts on how to make things better. On how to help others. On what direction he wanted to help his community grow. These thoughts were always there but with age came the time to approach them and the unbusy mind to figure them out. Those where the moments that felt great. He grew to appreciate the drive and motivation which was born in these moments.

Scott couldn't help but think it came down to perspective. A new way to look, a different view. It was a lot like climbing the hills out behind his childhood home. From the bottom you could see the top. You could see all the obstacles, the trails, and barriers that surrounded you. Once you reached the top of the hill there was a clarity of space. No longer were you standing at the foothills looking up. You could see the distance that lay before you and feel the world around you. Nothing changed, but with the new perspective Scott could see so much more of the world around him. Aging was a lot like that. He was reaching the pinnacle of his hill and he could see much more.

With this new perspective came appreciation of life. It started by watching people his own age dying. He wasn't thinking about the death in the usual way. Actually, he wasn't thinking about death at all. Instead the thoughts came from what it meant to be alive. The purpose of life. What did it mean to live each day? Now, more times than not, he would be grateful to be alive and experiencing what was in the present. The future would bring what it would bring. There was a simple type of freedom in that. The anxiety of youth took a long pause.

He approached the world differently. A lifelong hunter and fisherman, not for the sport of it, but for being able to put food on the table. It was both entertainment and a way of providing. He still loved to hunt. Scott still loved to be on the water and fish. This did not change. What changed was the appreciation for the life he was taking. He always respected and appreciated the animals that became food for his family, but now he could see the life he took was part of his own. The same life blood that coursed through his body. It was a connection that was deeper than youthful eyes could see. It was survival. It was food. It was a circle of life that all living things were a part of.

The most surprising, Scott found that he had gained coordination with age. It is true his body couldn't do all that is used to, but the things he could do were more precise. He had control that comes from years of muscles memory and practice of motion. When he would golf with Frank, he couldn't hit the ball 280 yards

The Scent of White

like his son did, but Scott could make that ball dance like only someone with years of experience had the control of body. When he was in the shop, a steady practiced hand showed the craftsmanship of unhurried age. Life coordinated and so did his body.

Wisdom and age must be shared. Scott and Mary took more time out together to talk. The lust of youth had turned into intimacy between two people. Not just physical intimacy, but intimacy that comes from years of shared thoughts, ideas, and feelings. True intimacy that a couple being close can share.

Sharing thoughts went farther than just the two of them. Scott found he was taking more time for morning coffee with friends. He would discuss ideas, not just the weather. It was important to share thoughts and compare experiences. Of course, that didn't leave out the bad jokes and bullshitting just for the sake of it. His friends, there was a connection that comes through growing old together that is a shared experience. The deeper level of connection from those sharing a bond of life.

It is more challenging to share that wisdom with youth. Well, that is not entirely true. Scott knew that a careful seed planted in the mind of youth would grow, but a tree could not be planted alone. He still volunteered to coach youth sports. He tried to be active in his community. And a part of his activity was to share his experience and thoughts with younger generations.

There was not pretentiousness in his actions. Instead it was time spent planting those seeds in fertile minds. Giving them thoughts that may get jumbled as often busy minds do, but also sowing the ideas that could help shape them into young men and women who were given a gift of experience.

Aging might have its limitations. There are many things that can be mistaken, misconstrued, or driven to be the hardships that come with age. The gift in aging comes from being able to live another day. Being able to watch children grow into adults. The peace of finding comfort in yourself and who you are. The growth from no longer caring or carrying the anxiety and stress of life. Being able to truly be yourself in the face of the things that you face on a daily basis.

Scott knew he had been given this gift. It was for a reason. Not a reason that could be defined but it was a gift none the less. There was no regret in how he spent his youth. There was reflection. But for him, being able to grow old, to see these things happen before him outweighed any prior misgivings. The hardships that came from aging were tiny specks of discomfort in what was to be an experience that he would not have

The Scent of White
changed. Yes, being 60 years old had its limitations, but being 60 years old reflected on a lifetime of growth, love, and life that were all the best parts.

Chapter 15: Dying part 8

Oh, rest. Finally, I feel rest. Where did it come from? Did the reverend calm my mind once again? Did I accept my position? I have no idea, but as my eyes open, I can feel rest again. Is this what healing feels like, or is it death? I have no idea, but I would trade all the last hours, all the last days to feel like this again. How long has it been anyway?

As my eyes are opening all I can see is light. But it is not the hospital lights. It is not the light that is coming through the windows. It is my light. My other sense of being. What I have lived my life for. Red eyed, blood shot as all hell. Disheveled. There SHE is. The one. There is Mary.

Mary, how much I have needed you. I know you have been here, but where have you been? I know you wouldn't leave my side. I know I haven't always been able to see you. But you are here. My soul could feel you. All those thoughts I had about my soul. Pure bullshit. I have always been connected to my soul because I could feel it with you.

The nurses looked through me. Almost past me. The doctors too. Even Frank and Heather had trouble seeing me. I didn't feel seen until that reverend. But the way he saw me pales in comparison to the way you see

The Scent of White

me. You look into my eyes, but you can see through that window, can't you? You see directly into the deepest parts of my being. I can't explain that connection. I can't explain that vulnerability of being so intimately connected to one person.

Mary, do you know you are the only person who has been in this room that hasn't said a word. We don't need words. Sure, when nerves come to light, I am sure you are talking everyone's ear off. I have seen you do it! But here, in the room with just us, there is no need to say a word. My heart can feel every single thought on your mind. And what a beautiful mind it is. So full of joy, light, passion, contentment. It is the mind that I have been lucky enough to know for oh so long.

I don't want to leave you Mary. I don't. I want to stay here with you and live another lifetime with you. It might be nonsense. It might be silly. But I would trade the world to go through this life with you again. I wouldn't change a thing. Just experience every second with you.

You give me serenity. I couldn't imagine doing this without you. I fear that if it is my time, you will have to go through this without me. I don't want that. I can't control that, but I don't want it. Bring me back with you Mary. By your side. Never in front. Never behind. But by your side for always more. That is the position that I took and the position I always want to be in.

What have you heard Mary? Communicate it to me. First the kids. All the staff. The reverend. This might be the real end. Right? Is that why you are all sad. They won't talk to me. They try. But they can't see me like you can. They just look through me. I might get a few details. But it is clinical. I want what you have to say. I want to hear everything from you.

Mary if it really is my time to go, I want you to know that you were the missing part of me. I may have been complete alone, but I am much bigger and more finished with you in it. You are that Mary. Please feel my thoughts like I feel yours. If it is my time, you need to know that. You need to feel that.

You will be strong. I have no doubt of that. You will lead our family like you always have. All those people talking about being equal. I could never equal you. You are so much more. Your vision. Your strength. Your light. It I has always been so much greater than my own, and I was allowed the privilege to live in that light Mary. Hear that from me.

I am imperfect. We all are. You see past those imperfections in me. You see all the potential that was there for us and you grew that. You nurtured that. I am

The Scent of White

not scared about where I am anymore. I know that you are going to join me on this journey and the next. It is there for all time. I appreciate you. I have always tried to live up to showing you all that you deserve. I know I came up short so often, but the look of how much you appreciated the effort made me want to be better, to try harder for you.

Every single time I have been here I have woken up with questions. I don't have questions now. I have you here and all I want is to communicate what you mean to me. What you have always meant. That is what I have left in me now. I hope that you can accept that one final gift that I have to give you.

I am not tried. Just stay here with me. Hold my hand just like you are now. Let's just be. Just be here together and share that intimacy that we always have. In my mind we will be holding each other's hand out on the water. Slowly drifting along. Taking in the sites. Floating in our favorite place. You know the one. It is the one that we picked together on our lake. The place we have shared so much. Go there with me Mary. Take that trip with me.

I'll be damned. I am not thirsty anymore.

Chapter 16: 2002

There is something special that happens when two people meet for the first time. There is a connection, a spark, a simple feeling that there is a need to find out more. The courting process could be labeled as an event. Then marriage is the next benchmark. It is emotional magic that only the two people partaking in it can know.

Families grow. There are births, and there are deaths. Things change. Often this overshadows the biggest change, growth. Since 1978 Scott and Mary had been growing independently every day, regardless of how out of tune it was to them at the time. That independent growth also meant that there was growth that was happening as a couple. The term soulmates is overused at the least, but being able to grow independently and find, accept, and appreciate that growth in another's soul is real existence.

For the first years of marriage and the birth of their family life was a blur for both Scott and Mary. They were so busy with chores and their growing clan that they couldn't stop for a minute of rest. Raising a family, then the endless school and sporting events gave little time for thought. The time spent making sure everyone was cared for and provided for, left both Scott and Mary tired and reliant on routines.

The Scent of White

Routine can be a good thing. Scott found it so easy to go through day to day life. He had his routine. Mary had a routine. Both kids had a routine. Mostly these routines overlapped and intertwined, but never slowed down enough to take stock of who they were becoming. It was easy, without these routines it would have been impossible to stay on top of their life and tend to their responsibilities. All these things are there for a reason, and there is a sense of accomplishment in each one.

The realization came on a Saturday night. Both Frank and Heather were out with friends, they were old enough to be out in vehicles and doing what all teenage kids do. The chores were all done. It was one of the first times in years that everything was taken care of and Scott and Mary had an entire evening together without the responsibilities of the world. Not as if they didn't go on dates and treat each other well, but this was outside of the routine. There was no need to plan a night out. It just happened.

The argument started as most do, over something completely inconsequential. Mary wanted to go out for a cocktail and a night of dancing. Scott wanted to stay home and watch a movie. It was just a simple decision of what to do with this spontaneous night alone. Two separate ideas that were both something they had done in the past and things they both enjoyed. Yet these ideas that couldn't be farther apart in motivation.

Scott had grown to enjoy familiarity. The home they built together. The space that they were alone and separated from the world. On a free night why would he want to be anywhere else. Mary loved all those things too, but she had grown a need to get out of those same walls she loved and reclaim that feeling of being free; surrounded by people, laughter, and fun away from the familiarity.

Logical minds would have said it was an easy compromise, or maybe even doing both. Like arguments have a tendency to do, what started out as a simple disagreement turned into bottled up feelings that had not been expressed or communicated. Sometimes simply because there is not time, sometimes because it is too complicated to put into words. Either way, all of those bottled up feelings began to come out in the worst way possible. Words being used to hurt. Feelings being expressed in frustration rather than communication.

In the end there was no dancing. In the end there was no movie. In the end there were only two people that were hurt, mad, and frustrated that their

The Scent of White

partner could not provide the needs that they never expressed. In the big scheme of things this argument was nothing special. It was not the start of a divorce or divide. They still loved each other. They still cared for each other. This was a small little event in a much bigger world they had built.

The only reason that this argument stands out at all is it was the first time Scott was scared. Afterward, he had gone out to the shop as he was known to do. It was under the disguise of working on some project that he would immediately have to invent, but in reality, it was his space where he could sort out his thoughts. At first it was frustration and anger. All the things he should have said flooded his mind. The ways that he could have attacked and scored a win, as if there could be a winner in an argument. Then came sadness. The reflection of all the ways he had hurt her. The regret of saying and doing things that he knew were far from true. Then forgiveness. For the things Mary had said, for the argument, and finally for himself. It was different each time, but these were always the elements that came to him.

The difference was this time there was a new feeling after forgiveness. This time he was afraid. True, there were only a few fights between he and Mary. The hurt and anger were always extremely short lived and never meant anything more than a difference in opinion. This time it felt different. Scott had realized that they had both grown, and some of that growth had not been in the same direction. They had become different people in many ways. It was the result of aging and learning more about who they were as individuals. They still had desires and needs, and the busy routines had hidden that those desires and needs had changed over time.

But if they had grown in different directions, what did that mean for the future. This was just one night alone. What would happen as the kids aged? What would happen when they had more free time with each other? Would they become roommates with nothing left in common? Or even worse. These were the questions that plagued him that night, and truth be told, many nights after. One of the biggest issues was the questions couldn't be answered overnight, or maybe questions that could not be answered at all.

Scott had always been a straight-line thinker. There was a problem, then you find a solution. You work for that solution, and if there is an issue you find a new path and start over. It is strait line. When you started with questions that did not have a solution, or at least one that couldn't be seen, that is when he had a

The Scent of White

problem. His thoughts would spin, his mind wouldn't rest. There was no solution. There were many things he could think about, and many actions he should take when he recognized this growth in different directions. However, it was not a solution.

For a time, issues seemed to pop up more and more. Not the arguments and fights, but Scott started to realize the more he took time to pay attention, Mary had changed. Once completely free spirited, she had become more structured and methodical in her thoughts and actions. She had taken enjoyment in new activities. Her social group had changed from wild and free to book clubs and social hours more and more. She had developed new habits. She was a brand-new person.

How had he gone that long without noticing? Were they too busy that they never noticed they had changed into different people? Between 2002 and 2003 he could not believe how wide his eyes had been opened to all the little things that had changed and happened between the two of them. From the outside he knew this would sound bad, he was noticing all this late. How could he see it when each day was still filled with all the good of their lives together? It was just a realization that life had been changed right beneath their feet when they were busy living.

Everything came to a head on October 17th. Both Scott and Mary were passionate about participating in their community, and when they could they would be involved in charities and events that were important to them. The one event that was never missed was the Our Cause is Paws fundraiser. Both passionate about dogs, they never missed this fundraiser for their local animal shelter. They went every year without fail regardless of sickness, responsibilities, or other events that may arise. It was tradition for a cause and would be a night filled with dinner, conversation, and dancing. A perfect night out.

The kids were both taken care of and out with friends on their own night of fun. Scott had finished getting ready early, but instead of plopping down in front of the TV or fussing with the million other little things to do, he went upstairs to their shared master bathroom. He wanted to talk to Mary while she got ready.

Even being a strong and independent woman like she was, Mary still fussed over traditional looks. So much pressure is pushed on women to look younger, with a perfect figure, and to meet the standards of beauty that had been preached to them. Mary knew

The Scent of White
this was all ridiculous, but she would spend an hour making sure she looked her best. If you asked her the reasons, she could never tell the whole story. It was something personal and cultural. It was a part of who she was.

As Mary fixed her hair, Scott knew that she was always a little shy about the gray that now streaked her golden locks. When she was younger, she always wore her hair long. A beautiful golden blonde with a natural curl that framed her face so amazingly well that you couldn't help but notice. Now there were traces of gray throughout. She had given up on trying to cover all the gray with dye years ago. There was just too much maintenance to keep up with. Now her hair was the same golden blonde, but in her eyes, you could see the age of years that had slipped away. Slightly shorter she felt that you couldn't quite see the shine that was once there. Scott knew he had given her many of these gray hairs. And no matter what she thought, he couldn't find one inch that didn't shine with the beauty from within.

As Scott watched he move on to her makeup. Mary seemed to fret over covering up all the little wrinkles. She thought of the age that shown with each crease and thought her skin had seemed to droop a bit now days. But Scott had seen each one of those wrinkles appear after years of laughter and tears. The experience of a life well lived. Her face didn't show the youthful glow, but instead showed a far greater awe of their shared life. All the things she had given up and had given to everyone else instead of herself.

Mary would twiddle with her dress. Her once slim and slightly hourglass figure now more filled out. She would remark about how the dress just didn't fit right and try to find the hidden figure that she once had. But that youthful body had given birth to two children. Her figure now shown that of a mother and the strength that comes with. Each day more defined by who she was and the things she enjoyed.

When she stood up and faced Scott there was a question in her eyes. Almost one of uncertainty. The question of do I look good enough. The question of am I enough? It was so silly. She was confident and strong in ways that were far beyond Scott, and in her day to day life that confidence was exuberant in the way she carried herself. Each time she spoke, you could hear it clearly. It was moments like this, preparing for her husband and friends, that all the insecurities surfaced.

It really was the first time in years that Scott had taken the time to watch all that she went through. It was the first time that he had noticed the insecurities surface in her. It was the first time that he had seen HER

The Scent of White

in a long time. And it broke his heart a little. This was the moment it came to a head.

When she faced him, it literally took his breath for a moment. She was spectacular. Her hair in a perfect style to frame a face that had only gotten prettier with time to him. Her body was the place he had turned for acceptance, love, and warmth. It had developed with many shared experiences and had grown their family. Their world. She was the world to him. And all he could see was pure beauty. A creature that was hard to take in with just the naked eye.

Beauty. Beautiful. There are so many ways to use this word. While the definition is always similar, it is never used correctly. In youth it is nearly always purely physical. During courting it can be used as a compliment or to evoke an emotion. It can be used to be manipulative. It can be a word that becomes an unattainable standard for people to try and live up to. While the factual definition of the word may agree, it is not the proper use.

In that moment Scott understood beauty in a way that many people will forever miss. Beauty doesn't come from the outside, beauty comes from within. It is the character, ideas, and soul. It is the person that shines through the exterior. It is the life they have lived.

It is the life that has been shared. It is all the intangible things that can never be defined by a quick look. That is what makes a person beautiful. And in that moment, he saw just how beautiful Mary was.

It had come to a head. In that simple moment, his worry and fear had seemed to fade away in an instant. No matter how shallow it seemed, it took that moment of seeing through all those insecurities and seeing the beautiful woman that stood before him begging acceptance on a level so much more primal. The question was not how do I look. The question was am I enough for you. It was the moment that thunder rained down from above on his mind.

For just a moment she was trying to reclaim part of who she used to be, but she didn't need to. Today she was so much more than she had been then. Scott had loved and appreciated her more today than yesterday, and the same would be true tomorrow. She had grown and changed physically, which brought more beauty and appreciation. Why would recognizing her emotional and ideological change be any different? It symbolized all the growth they shared. It took him until that October evening to realize that he loved every moment of growth and change she could ever present. They had grown and changed together, and neither would be under appreciated again.

The Scent of White
    It is said that we will all change into five completely different people in our lives. Some of those people we have already been, and some are left to change into. But we share those changes with the person that accepts, loves, and appreciates us not for only who we were, but who we are becoming. It may have taken years for Scott to see this for the first time, but that day he vowed to always try and stay in the present with Mary. Each version they had yet to become would be a brand-new life to live together.

Chapter 17: Dying part 9

Well Shit. This really can't be good. I feel a little better.

My eyes seem to focus a lot faster now. I know where I am. I feel better. I feel at peace. It must be a sign of something. What is it?

Again, take stock. I was just here with Mary. She was holding my hand. I wasn't tired. I just wanted to stay with her. It was going to be just us for a bit. A shared moment with her. She was with me. That is all that mattered. So why when I opened my eyes is everyone here.

Frank. On my left. He always stands at the right side of the family. My Mary. She is in the middle. Heather is on the right. They are all hugging.

Up until now I have always had people checking on me. One by one they have come in. They have been here for me. Helping to get better. Helping me feel safer. Helping me understand. So why are they all here now? All together. It felt as if I just shut my eyes. How did they all get here so fast? I really wasn't tired. Did I fall asleep again? Did they put me out? Maybe it will always be a mystery. Their eyes are red. They have been crying. I can tell that. The sadness is written on faces like it was painted on there.

The Scent of White

What is happening? Something is different. It is more of a feeling. I can't really describe it. Maybe my mind is playing tricks because they are all here at once. But it does feel different. Is it a cloak has been draped over everyone? It doesn't feel good. Not really a bad feeling either though. But there is something else different.

They see me. Mary has always seen me. The Reverend seemed to see me too. Now they all see me. Their eyes are giving it away. They are looking deeper into me. Not my crippled-up body this time. They see through the window. I don't think that is what is causing this feeling.

The pace is slower. The nurses and doctors had already slowed down from the fever pitch they were racing when I first woke up. Now it is as if they have become snails moving. Just doing things ideally as they move from one place to the next. More routine than before. It feels methodical but practiced. Slow. I still don't think that is making me feel different.

Touch! That is it. Touch is different. The nurses are touching my family. Almost sympathetically as they go on with their tasks. There are hands on shoulders. There is compassion. The robotic eyes they had moving through the room now are filled with emotion. It as though they are sharing in the grief. Something they must go through each day, but through compassion they feel again and again. They breath with the family. That touch wasn't there before. That is different.

It can't bode well for me. I know that. But what does it mean? Am I dead and I don't know it? Is this the part where my guards start calling out dead man walking? Is my recovery going to be called a miracle at this point? The worst part about being trapped like this is the total lack of understanding. They talk past me. They move past me. I don't understand it at all.

I should be afraid. I am not. It is still peaceful in here. I can't explain it. I feel it though. It is definitely there. It is funny, family is all around me, but I think I am dying alone. I am the only one going through this.

There is more. More people. Funny, I know they are family too. Too distant. I can't even think about names. I can't even figure out who they are. They are there, around me. I can see them. They may be family, but I don't feel the presence of them in the room like my family. The family before me. I get that. I can understand what they are to me. Maybe that is the important part. That is what they need.

I know I am observing everything happening, but it feels like I am seeing it from a distance. I kind of

The Scent of White

am. I can't move. They have no idea where I am. I have no idea how long I have been here. I am just an observer in an otherwise turning world. How odd is that? I don't know where this came from. I guess it is just who I am now. There is no rhythm to this place. It is just being.

I know one thing. I don't want this. I want my family out living. I want them to have adventures. Stop. It is like someone hit stop on life for everyone around me, myself included. Life shouldn't stop for me. Celebrate me. Live the life I want to live. I will meet you in that life. I am there. I am always there.

I have been so thirsty, but now it comes and goes. I still want some water, but it is fading now. It is more of my soul that needs a drink, I think. That nurse is putting something more in me. I wonder if I will remember anything at all.

Chapter 18: 2019

Cool. Crisp. Scents. All the things that make fall great were in the air. Scott always loved the fall. It was the time of year that he could feel good. The air cooled down from the intense heat of summer. Nights were still long enough to enjoy being outdoors. The scent of fall was still his favorite. The whole world changed color. There was nothing better than this time of year, and that was a fact.

Over the past few years he had taken up walking everyday as a point of health. It had started after a routine doctor's visit. A visit that was brought on by the aging process. This time when the results came back with higher cholesterol, elevated blood pressure, and a higher risk for heart disease, something needed to change. All terms that came expectedly with getting older, but words that started to take meaning when you want to keep living a life that you love.

Scott and Mary always had dogs around the house. Sometimes it was one, and even once had climbed up to four at once. Having them around was something both loved. The concept of taking walks wasn't unheard of, but for most of the years, time was a factor. What could have been long walks usually turned into short jaunts around the block, or once the yard was fenced, less walks and more opening the door.

The Scent of White
Now with a plethora of free time, and his health on the line, walks took on a new meaning. His current dog ranger always provided motivation to leash up and head out. The choice was easy. Better eating. More conscious about healthy choices. And best of all, in Ranger's eyes, was a nightly walk. That would be his plan for a longer life, and more discovery.

Often Mary would join in on the hikes around the lake home. It started with just walking up and down the streets. Stopping to talk with the neighbors. Exploring paths. Finding overgrown routes to new areas. It started off as a chore, but the more that they explored, the more adventures they started to have. They began to really notice all the beauty in where they lived, and all the places left undiscovered for too long.

During the hot summer months there would be stops at the boat landing to let ranger off leash to go for a refreshing swim in the lake. To him, it must have been a life changing difference to the lake at home. Ranger had inspired exploration, never seeming to tire of finding something new or different and always ready for the next round.

During the spring it would be constant stops to see the buds on the trees. Time spent taking in the smells of rebirth. They would always stop on the gravel trails and make little rivers for the water to drain off the path into the surrounding areas. They would take the longer path each and every time, just looking for all the spots winter was slowly releasing her hold on the earth.

The winters were longer. Cold weather would shorten the walks a bit. Still adventurous, Scott would put on his skis or snowshoes and start across an ice-covered lake to take in the sites from a perspective that could not be seen at such a slow pace during the other seasons. These were always Ranger's favorite walks. Completely free and off his leash he could run until his heart was content. He could explore his own path, but always return to lead the pack across the frozen ground.

All the seasons leading up to fall. There was always something far more special about the fall walks. They would see the colors change before their eyes. The world would change anew each day, even when they took the same path. From the campfires, to the last BBQs of the season, it would fill the senses only the way this season could. It was a time that everyone seemed to take stock of their lives and prepare for the long winter that was to come. They would soak up the last fleeting moments of the warm weather and spending time with family and friends.

Scott and Mary were always active in the community. They spent time at community events. They

The Scent of White

tried to stay in touch with their neighbors, even hosting dinners for guests from their old neighborhood. They cherished the community and believed beyond a doubt that community was the foundation.

It wasn't until he started walking that Scott really got to know the community. It was more than the frequent stops to say a quick hi to everyone that happened to be outdoors at the time. He could also be a spectator taking in the events happening at each house he passed. There were constant changes. Decorations going up. Families growing. It was taking in the community from an observer's perspective. He could see the community become alive and seemingly breath with the seasons. All the time spent prior in community events paled to knowing his neighbors now.

The walks had worked. By his next yearly checkup Scott was almost "in shape" again and had even been listed as optimal in all of the benchmark health standards. Aside from his health, the walks had awakened him, and he felt reconnected. Not just to the community and neighborhood, but also, he had met himself again. There was a longing he didn't know he had, but it was to learn about himself. Walking may have been the key to getting back into shape, but also his mental capacity had been reconditioned.

Tuesday, November 19th started off like any other day. Scott and Mary had woken up to have a coffee on the front porch. The weather was beautiful and watching the sun rise over the lake from the porch had developed into a regular morning occurrence. Scott had brought his laptop out with him so that he could check up on the local news for the day. It had become the routine on the nice mornings. The kitchen bar would suffice for the days that weren't so nice.

After a morning coffee and talk about life with Mary, he knew that there were some projects waiting. The tasks were never ending. This time of year, it was getting ready for winter. Making sure the lawn was up to par and fertilized for the season. The summer toys needed to be winterized and put away. There were tasks around the house, around the yard, and just a process of getting ready for what was to come. But with the slower pace of retirement, these tasks would stretch out over weeks instead of a quick night or two.

After a morning working in the yard, 11 am had snuck up on him in no time at all. Eleven bells was lunch time now. It is funny, the older he had gotten, mealtimes were getting earlier and earlier. And his body had demanded he stop now for a quick bite. One of his great pleasures of late was to wash up and make lunch for himself and Mary. He had always loved to cook and

The Scent of White

even a quick sandwich for lunch brought him joy, even more so to share it with her.

The day was too nice not to take some time for play too. Mary had a bookstore event and was headed into town for the afternoon, so shortly after noon he and Ranger were sitting in the boat casting a line. Even if the fish were not biting, it was more important to make the open water last as long as possible. There was something divine about sitting on the open water in the warm breeze from the fall winds that brought his life into perspective and filled him with a joy beyond words. A few fish later, and after a refreshing afternoon, they headed into the docks to show off their catch.

No time for fresh fish tonight. It was family dinner night. It seemed impossible with so many schedules to consider, but over the past year they had made a family pact. At least once every other week they would get together and have a meal together. Sometimes it was quick, sometimes it would last all night, but there would always be a family dinner. They would never leave the table until the date of the next dinner was set. It was a way of keeping them all connected.

This family dinner would be a little different. More often than not, Scott and Mary would cook together and serve a new dish for the family at the lake house. Sometimes the kids would host. And at the rarest of times they would go out to a local bar or restaurant to take in something different. Tonight would be one of those nights they would go out on the town. This time of year was always busy, and not having to choose what to cook or make it a rush, the local family diner was a great option. It seemed fitting.

By seven o'clock that night they were back home having set the next date for ten days out. It was a great time but walking through the door there was something evident right away. Ranger was sitting, leash by his side, at the door. He always knew when it was time to take a walk. It had become his routine. Tail wagging a million miles a minute and ready for another adventure. Mary would not go with today. She had her own things to tend to. Scott and Ranger leashed up and it was off for another trip.

Some of the best walks were the ones taken without a plan. They would start out the door and let the path take them on a journey. It was as random as it sounded. By this time, they had explored nearly every inch of the land, but each walk would be a new adventure. They started off toward an old favorite. It was a trip down a path that had been haphazardly cut to the lake. The trail was about two miles long and

The Scent of White
would take almost an hour to walk, but it was beautiful being near the lake nearly the entire time and weaving in and out of private property as they passed through the communal land.

The best part of the trip was the halfway point. There was an old basswood tree right off the beach that seemed a thousand years old. Tall and big, it had trunks heading out all in different directions that came from the same base. It looked as though seven trees had chosen to share the same footprint to overlook and protect the lake for all of time. It was a great spot to stop and rest as they prepared for the journey back home.

It was also the spot that Scott would stop and sneak a cigar from time to time. He was not sneaking anything. Mary knew about it, and really didn't mind. He just knew how much she hated the smell and thought this was the perfect spot to indulge and relax overlooking one of his favorite sites. It was a spot that felt like all his own, and it was only the special people in his life that he shared it with. Relaxing by the water, it would be just for him and Ranger. Two best friends sitting on the edge of a lake they both loved so much, taking a break from the world.

It was a short break, but one that couldn't have felt better in the cool fall air. The journey home had started uneventful. There was a fulfilling feeling that started each time they were walking, but there was also the feeling of another adventure coming to an end. A little sadness knowing it would be the end of another day. Even the gate of Rangers walk seemed to slow, not out of lack of energy, but trying to drag the pleasure out as long as possible. A cherishing of the time spent with a friend.

They had made it off the path with only about four blocks to go to make it back to the house. Such a great trip, but the entire way Scott had felt a little disassociated with himself. Part of the time feeling like he was floating, part of the time feeling like there was an aura around him. It wasn't like he had never felt similar, but something was a little different. He couldn't put his finger on it, but there was more.

Scott didn't remember twisting his ankle, but he must have. His left leg started to limp just a bit as he walked. It must have been injured when they took that last few steps off the trail. Oh well, it happens. But he could feel a light headedness that was coming and going, more things just out of place. Maybe he had injured it a little more than he thought. There must have been something that happened, a twist or

The Scent of White
something must have ran up his entire leg. The limp was worse. He felt worse. It wasn't a good feeling but by now there were only three blocks left.

Darkness.

No one had seen it happen. No one was really paying attention to an older man walking down the sidewalk, even though it was the neighbor they talked to a thousand times. It was a normal sight. No one would have noticed right away at all if it had not been for Ranger barking and running around erratically. All the neighbors knew Scott and Ranger. But mostly Ranger. He was the 'best boy' according to them all. Larry lived in the house where Scott had collapsed. Even though he didn't see, he knew Ranger would never be running around and rarely barked. He had to investigate more. When he went outside his first instinct was yell for help. Scott was just off the sidewalk. Not moving. Not awake.

Mike came out next. No one knew what happened. All they knew is that Scott was laying there and not moving. It was bad. The grass did get dewy this time of year as the high temps of the day cooled to the crisp night air. Maybe he had slipped. Maybe he had a heart attack. All they knew was he was not coming too,

All that was heard were the shouts of Mike and Larry to call an ambulance.

It might never be known which neighbor called the ambulance first, but it turns out several had. By this time a small crowd had gathered around to try and help. Scott was well known and liked by all he had met. Each heart sank a little lower the longer it took for him to awaken again.

The ambulance arrived. The medics worked fast. Before you could blink Scott had been loaded up and whisked away. The neighbors dispersed. Sarah, Larry's wife, grabbed Ranger and left to break the news to Mary. Laura, Mike's wife, went inside to call Frank and Heather. They were all known. They all had a place in this community. It was their home.

Sarah searched for the words as she approached the house. How could she tell Mary? It felt better to run the short distance than call, and of course there was Ranger. He seemed as confused as all the neighbors. The entire way he pulled as hard as he could to follow the direction of the ambulance. He wanted to go too. He knew something wasn't right.

Mary collapsed. The words were few, but the pit of her stomach let her know it wasn't good. It would be a day not forgotten. The forbearing feeling passed

The Scent of White
through her as much as anything else. Even with limited information, the part of you that fears the worst knows when a love one is in danger. Trust your gut. It is a cliché that proves to be true time and time again.

The drive to the hospital was quick. Speed limits had turned into suggestions as they often do during those moments. Sarah drove. Mary was in no condition. When they arrived, Scott was in an emergency room. They couldn't see what was happening, but they could hear. Doctors calling out orders for tests. Nurses running back and forth quicker than expected. You didn't need to know the details to feel the atmosphere in the room.

An hour had passed. Then almost two. There were only a few updates from doctors taking quick breaks. The words were always the same, he is stable. He is non-responsive. We don't know what is wrong. They are running tests. It was the same words, repeated over and over. The same feeling. At least he was stable. How little relief that brought was amazing, but it was still relief. There was hope. You need to cling on to that hope with both hands. Frank and Heather had arrived. They were all waiting. A few neighbors had drifted in. It was turning into a gathering.

By the third hour there was no more the emergency room could do. There were some whispers about a stroke, but no one really knew what had happened. All they knew is the emergency room had done all they could. He was stable. The tests were being ran. The ICU had a bed open. That is where he belonged, in the hospital with a doctor more specialized in running his case. There was no choice, that is what was going to happen.

By the time the doctors could sit with Mary and explain the details to the best of what they knew, it was after midnight. They were all emotionally and physically exhausted. It had been a trying time and an emotional one for sure, but it also was a shake up in the routine. The doctor had come in and had checked in with Mary. After explaining what information they had, he had asked one last question, "Can you tell me anything you can remember about what he was doing?"

"It was just a walk." Was all she could muster.

The Scent of White
Chapter 19: Revelations

I know I am not awake, but I know I am not asleep either. Is it a dream? Have they given me more medications that are keeping me in this state? What is happening is bizarre. I can't feel myself, but I have so much clarity in my thoughts. There are many feelings. So much has happened. So much has changed. Is this death?

I know one thing. I am vulnerable. For the first time in my adult life, I am completely vulnerable. I require help to live. I require help to breath. I need to have someone here for every single action. The only thing that I own are my thoughts. It is the only thing that I have left. Complete vulnerability.

Maybe this is the start of something great. The one thing that I have learned in my time on this earth is that the greatest accomplishments of my life have come from vulnerability. It is when I have let my guard down and taken a risk that I grew. It is then when things had started to change and led to accomplishments. Of course, there are a lot of risks that come with it too.

When we are vulnerable, we can be hurt. We can fail. We can be crushed. Our guard is down, and we are opening ourselves up to anything. We can risk everything we have and come up short. The results are not always in our favor.

But if we are not willing to risk ourselves, if we are not willing to take a chance, nothing will ever change. Being stagnate leads to nothing. It is really one of those lessons that scares us. To learn that to be great we must take the chance. We must risk all the negative outcomes in order to go beyond our past. That is the definition of being vulnerable. It is the definition of what makes the difference between living the life we desire and the life of our dreams in exchange for the comfort of being in a box where we are guarded every day. Maybe this is the start of the next great thing. Total vulnerability leading to total greatness.

My greatest accomplishments. It's not what I thought it would be. I have had so much time to sit and reflect. Think about life. My thoughts been a part of everything that has happened. There have been a lot of accomplishments in my life and I feel good about that.

I have maintained a great job. I have made plenty of money to provide for my family to buy items that could be called luxury anywhere else. I have built a woodshop and created art. I have been able to learn more about the world, building, and repairing than I ever thought I would. I have owned things I have really wanted. I have set goals. I have built and accomplished

The Scent of White

those goals in a way that others don't understand. I have spent time traveling the world. I have developed new ways to approach ideas and tasks. Every single day I have tried to be better than the person that I was the yesterday. So much of my life I have spent trying to accomplish and do all that I can and to achieve. Those are all accomplishments of my life.

But none of it, absolutely none of it means a damn right now. Those accomplishments pale in comparison to the life I have been given the opportunity to live. I have been given the opportunity to grow personally. I have been given the time to develop and change as I face challenges. I have allowed myself the time to process who I am and live a life true to who I want to be.

I have lived a life filled with values and morals. I have set a path that I believe was right and did my best to live up to those ideals. I am not perfect. There was the vision to see my imperfections and work to make those imperfections better. I have slipped. There are times that I have not lived up to who I am and who I should be.

But the greatest accomplishment, the thing that as occupied every inch of my being during this time, has been my family. My mother and father. My wife. My children. Family has been the most important part of my life. This is the reason that all the rest of my accomplishments have existed. It has been for them that I have tried to be better, that I have tried to do more. It is the family that has been in my life, that has meant more to me, than anything else. It is them that I chose to be constantly vulnerable to. They were my greatest risk and my greatest accomplishment.

There were so many times that life got in the way of realizing that. I let my life, the responsibilities, the chores, the mundane day to day life take over. It has only been during these last few years when I gained perspective and taken the time to appreciate the gift that I have been given, a long life to appreciate them. Time slips away over the moments of our lives right behind our closed eyelids. Every blink revolves a second, a minute, an hour, a day, a lifetime.

We are tasked with the ability to appreciate a life well lived, but so often we forget to appreciate each blink. Each passing moment. Each mundane task. When I was allowed the perspective to slow down and just be, the most mundane becomes the most important. Sharing a simple meal. Getting the mail. Sharing in a laugh. Those are the passing quiet moments that have meant the most.

The Scent of White

These are the thoughts I have chosen to think about. This time, the time I have been here with nothing to do but be, they are the dreams that have intertwined in my being. The house, the cars, the money, the possessions, everything that I have worked for have not entered my thoughts at all. I have thought about my dogs. I have thought about who I have become. I have thought about my family. The moments that have built a life. These are the things that I want to be remembered for. When my life is summed up in a dash between the years of my birth and death, I don't want to be remembered for what I had or meaningless accomplishments. Even the things I didn't do won't be remembered. Those things are inconsequential and will fade away. They are things that will not mean a damn to anyone and will be forgotten tomorrow.

I want a legacy. My legacy is to live on in the people's lives I have touched. In that sense I will live forever. The youth that I have reached out to. My friends. My neighbors. And most of all my family. The simple pleasure of being chosen to be in someone's life because they chose to have me there. The effect that I had on them no matter how big or small. That is the legacy I want to live in. The stories that are told. The memories that were made. The changes in hearts and minds of friends. There is no greater legacy to be had.

Chapter 20: Rebirth

Awake.

My head is clear. I don't know why, but I can feel again. I can see clearly. The last few hours were a dream. Well, not really a dream. I don't know what that was. Reflection. Rebirth. I don't know.

It is so peaceful here. My family. They are here. I can see them, but more importantly I can feel them. I can feel each moment they are with me, willing me to get better. It is the weirdest feeling, but it is unbelievably comforting.

I can hear them speak; I don't know what words they are choosing. I don't know why. They are just that words. Nothing more, words. They are as much being said to comfort the living as they are for me. At this point, words offer me no comfort. I am sure that if I heard clearly, I would find some comfort, but right now they are meaningless.

I feel light. I am content. I feel fulfilled. All that is important to me is surrounding me. I have lived a good life. I have had so many more moments that were good than bad. So many experiences. My life was lived for something more important than myself. That is contentment. I have fulfilled a purpose.

The Scent of White

Nurses. They are coming and going. I think they are there to comfort my family. That is how is seems. Mindlessly looking at monitors. Speaking soft words to all of them around. They are there for them, not for me anymore. Sure, they are pushing some concoction into my veins. I don't know. I can't even feel it. I am not sleepy anymore. I don't know what the effects are, but I can't honestly feel like it changes anything. There is clarity.

Doctors. I haven't seen them in a while. I am sure they will be by soon. What is the point? Why check on me? I am sure they have done all they can. There isn't a need to watch a man that isn't changing. They can still help others. But a man in stagnation doesn't have many options left. They have priorities, and I don't need to be one.

Dying.

That is not a question anymore. How else do you explain it? I haven't made any improvements. But for the first time I am calm. I have been given a gift of clarity. The drugs are not affecting my mental state, but I feel at peace. My thirst has been quenched. Is it the end? Is it the beginning? I don't have the answers, but for some reason I don't really care.

The one last great experience. So many times you hear that we only live once. That is complete bullshit. We live every day. Every day we wake up and get to reinvent ourselves. We get to have new experiences. We get to live. The truth is that we live every day and only die once. I feel like embarking on this trip is momentary.

The words might not be affecting me but thank whatever God you believe in that I can still feel their touch. We have five senses, but the sense of touch stands out much more. From the time we are held as babies, the sweet cuddles from our youth, the touch of our partner, to the final touch of goodbye. We are driven, refreshed, and comforted by touch. It is the closest most intimate thing that you can feel from someone else. And I can feel their touches. As each family member holds my hand, rubs my head, or just brushes against me, I can feel each one. It is intimate. It brings love. Pure, unadulterated peace.

I can feel so much love coming from them. It feels like my entire world is one of love. I think I have been using peace wrong. It isn't necessarily peace that I feel, but love. Maybe they are one of the same. I can feel so much. From the presence of others in the room, to the hearts that have reached out to take care of me. The babies being born down the hall. There is love that

The Scent of White
surrounds me. It is the matter that makes up the world. Whether we are seeking it out or enveloped in it like I am now, there is no denying that energy.

Death.

I know my body is shutting down. I don't know how I know it, maybe my brain has a subconscious connection I can't explain, but I can feel it. This is death. It doesn't mean I can explain it, but I am oddly not confused. I can just feel it coming on. It is dark. It is light. It is nothing and everything all rolled into one. All I know is that it is coming for me. The grim reaper.

It is a gift. I know that sounds ridiculous, but these final moments of time is a great gift. It is the punctuation that serves to end all that has ever been. I have been given these last moments to say goodbye in some way. Maybe a slight consolation, but none the less it is precious to me. Maybe it would have been easier on them to not have to watch this. Not to have to feel all the pains of the day to day death that has progressed so slowly before them. They see death, I see the love one last time with total clearness of mind. Just as death will be a gift ending my life.

I can feel it starting to fade. My body that is. My thoughts are as clear as ever, but I can feel my paralyzed body giving out. It is like the fade out at the end of a movie. The projector light is still as bright as ever, but the screen is fading to black. My body is becoming black. The vessel that has carried me through this life, raised two children, spent so many hours contemplating is now becoming a shell that is no longer a part of me.

I don't know what is in store for me next. I am completely vulnerable, and the new great adventure that lays in wait will appreciate that vulnerability. Greatness. Whatever is to come, it must be a great chapter, regardless if it is blank pages, or a book that has already been written thousands of times over. It is progress and change. Something moving. Energy. Love. Contentment. Fulfillment. I feel them all now.

I am dead. I can see it on their faces. My last breath has gone. Their eyes are leaving me. How long will it be before my consciousness will fade away too? Or has it already? But in their eyes, I am dead. It is written as clear as day. Every tear. Every cry. It is one of longing and missing someone more than you could ever miss yourself. But I am still hear. I haven't left, and I will never leave. Maybe I will just live on in the passing memory that brings a spark to an eye. Or maybe I will live on in some other form far greater. But you will all be my legacy. It will be through you that I will never

The Scent of White

leave. Maybe forgotten after time, but with you I will live on.

    I am going now. It is enveloping me. Death that is. It feels as though I am laying on the edge of the water and the wind has just started to blow. A breeze that is carrying my existence on its every breath. At first there are only a few waves. I can feel them at my feet. As the breeze grows, so does the lapping waves as they procced up my body. Slowly sinking in the water that birthed me. Slowly until I can feel my entire being floating in the waves of all existence. My life, or what was my life is now one with it. Deeper and deeper into the water. I am becoming one with it. What started as a lapping at my toes has now enveloped me completely. No more floating. No more breeze. Just a liquid flow of everything that ever was and everything that will be.

    Complete.

    Energy.

Chapter 21: Remembrance

Scott (Scottie) Alan Larkin

Died today (11/26/2019). You may not have known him, but he made your world a better place to be in. A family man at heart, Scott spent his years as an electrician by trade, but as a man of the community by night. Raising his two children Frank (Elisabeth) and Heather (Ryan) kept him busy for many years. A devotion and constant love to his wife Mary who never left his side.

After a weeklong battle in the hospital, Scott finally had to say enough is enough. It is time for you all to get back to living. He let go. And the world will forever be a smaller place because of it.

Survived by his wife and children. Scott will be going to meet the rest of his family in the great here after. By Scott's specific request, there will be no funeral arrangements. However, if you would like to have a beer in his memory, there will be a gathering at Lucky's Tavern at 5 pm on Friday, November 29th. The first round is on him.